What are you wearing?

THE INSPIRATIONAL SPIRITUAL SIDE OF

Fashion

Compiled by: Chebra "OCHEA" Dorsey

HAVANA BOOK GROUP LLC
WWW.HAVANABOOKGROUP.COM

HAVANA BOOK GROUP LLC
43537 RIDGE PARK DRIVE
TEMECULA, CA. 92590

ISBN: 979-8-9891918-5-7

ICCI
Fashion Boutique

Introduction

In a world that is in a perpetual state of transformation, where cultures collide and trends evolve in the blink of an eye, one constant thread weaves its way through the fabric of our existence - fashion. More than just clothing and accessories, fashion is a language that speaks volumes about who we are, where we come from, and where we aspire to go. It is a universal art form that transcends time and boundaries, expressing individuality, creativity, and the collective spirit of humanity.

In the pages that follow, we embark on a journey to unravel the multifaceted tapestry of fashion, exploring not only the garments that grace our bodies but also the intricate emotions, histories, and aspirations they embody.

Fashion is far more than an arrangement of fabrics and adornments; it is a medium through which we communicate with the world. It is a silent statement that reflects our mood, personality, and values, often conveying messages that words cannot capture. From the flamboyant to the understated, from the avant-garde to the classic, each sartorial choice we make is an invitation for the world to perceive a glimpse of our inner selves.

This book is not just a catalog of trends, nor is it a rulebook for dos and don'ts. It is an exploration into the rich history of fashion and what it means to each contributing author. The chapters in this book go beyond the surface, beyond the glitz and glamour, to uncover the intimate relationship between fashion and our sense of self. You will explore how clothing can empower and embolden, how it can cradle memories and tell stories, and how it can forge connections that transcend language and geography. Through the exploration of history, culture, psychology, and creativity, we aim to reveal the true essence of fashion - a powerful force that shapes not only our appearances but also the narratives of our lives. So, fasten your seatbelt, for we are about to embark on a captivating odyssey into the heart and soul of what it truly means to be fashionable.

Remember always, you never get a second chance to make a great first impression. The embodiment of the "Ochea" brand is to always step out and show up in life as your true, authentic, unique, and amazing self. Share your fashion with the world.

Disclaimer: Dr Chebra Dorsey features her own exclusive designs and has included in the book fashions from other fabulous designers that she wishes to feature. Dr. Chebra enjoys recognizing other talented and creative designers. One of her greatest passions is to collaborate with others.

Foreword

It is with great excitement that I introduce to you Chebra Dorsey, affectionately known as "Ochea". This is a prominent lady who is the owner of Ochea Fashion Boutique located in Lemon Grove, CA. I am more than pleased to state that she is not only a LOANI Executive member but also a World Superhero. Blessed with a sharp eye for fashion, Ochea is well known for doing celebrity fashion shows. Her taste in fashion and design is flawless.

A native of San Diego, she commenced her career as a licensed Cosmetologist two decades ago but in the past decade has since moved into designing women's clothing for ladies across the globe. This amazing lady inspires women of all ethnic groups and sizes to feel free to be themselves. Her designs exude leadership and confidence and empower those who wear them. The way she arranges colors and styles makes the wearer of her clothing feel elegant, beautiful, and royal.

Among her clientele she counts actresses Wendy Lynn Adams and Kita Williams. These are just a few of her high-profile celebrity clients who love her designs. Her elegant beaded Roman Air Gown has been worn many times on the Beverly Hills Red Carpet Stage.

Ochea is indeed a spiritual being and is always happy to make other people happy. She is popular in her community. She has provided specialized hair services to former cancer patients who would have suffered hair loss due to chemotherapy and radiation treatments. Often Ochea sponsors the boys and girls club of San Diego, children's hospitals, and the food for children foundations.

She has done many sold-out fashion shows, and she is now a co-author who is currently writing her own book to be launched in August 2023. Ochea is a recipient of numerous awards for her dedication and work. Last year one of her awards was the IONIC Celebrity Designer award. The Multi-Cultural Motion Picture Association in Hollywood presented OCHEA with many prestigious awards over the years, including their highest Lady in Red award. She has received the Call to Service Award from two Presidents of the United States and numerous awards from the California State Senate and Assembly as well as local City and County officials for her dedication and commitment to women globally. She also received the Humanitarian Award 2021 and the 2021 Legendary Icon Designer Award.

In 2020 Ochea was asked to serve on the prestigious "She Inspires Me" Advisory Board." She Inspires Me" is a global organization that serves women all over the world; in addition, she was presented with one of the 2020 "She Inspires Me Awards". She is a co-author in a book called "Quarentena and Beyond", an International Book. In 2021 Ochea received the "Iconic Designer of the Year" award.

Ochea is grateful to God and the beautiful people in her life who are there every day for her and inspire her to live her dreams. An amazing fact is that there was a time she lost everything and was homeless living on the street but worked hard and brought herself back up to the top. What an amazing and resilient lady she is.

Professor Caroline Makaka. Founder of Ladies of All Nations International, Creator of We Are the Change Movement and Beautiful Survivor and Superhero Platforms, Educator, International Best-Selling Author/Speaker, Global Impact Leader and Humanitarian

Prof. Dr. Caroline Makaka

Chapter Overview

Dr. Angelica Benavides

Infusing Sensuality and Empowering Elegance

In the dynamic world of entrepreneurship, women are forging their paths with passion, determination, and style. This captivating synergy of business acumen and fashion prowess has given rise to a new era of empowered female leaders who recognize that how they present themselves can be a powerful extension of their brand identity.

It is time for a captivating exploration of the unique relationship between women entrepreneurs and the world of fashion. In this journey, we delve into the art of crafting a distinctive personal style that not only reflects business values but also exudes confidence, professionalism, and authenticity.

From the boardroom to networking events, from creative brainstorms to strategic partnerships, the way a woman entrepreneur dresses tells a story that resonates with clients, collaborators, and stakeholders. Through insightful discussions, expert advice, and inspiring stories,

In today's competitive business landscape, fashion plays a role in building a strong personal and professional image.

Fashion is vital in the business world because it has become significant for entrepreneurs in this era. Fashion conveys professionalism, brand identity, and confidence. A well-chosen style can enhance networking, make a lasting impression, and align with a company's values.

Even more, after you go through life challenges and struggle or let's say in the Dark Knights of the Soul, you also tend to find the best version of yourself. It is a perfect time to step into your power and re-identify the new you and new look. In my darkest moments, it is when I dared to be me and stepped into my new identity—not just a brand identity but daring to dress sexier and more sensual in a business way.

You see being a cancer survivor and losing parts of me took me to a place of feeling less beautiful and especially not sexy. But when I made a decision to just be "ME", it is when I tapped into a sense of sensual and sexy look into my business attire.

I invite you to celebrate the women who are breaking stereotypes, shattering glass ceilings, and making their mark as entrepreneurs while embracing the transformative power of fashion. Let's embark on a captivating journey where entrepreneurship meets elegance, sensuality, innovation, and style converges. Time to show up unapologetic!

If you are also embracing low self-confidence in your body, It's wonderful to embrace your personal style while navigating the business world. Here's how you can infuse sensuality into your business attire while maintaining professionalism:

1. Embrace Confidence: Your confidence is your greatest asset. Embrace your journey, and let your strength and resilience shine through in your demeanor and fashion choices.

2. Choose Empowering Silhouettes: Opt for tailored pieces that accentuate your figure in a way that makes you feel confident and comfortable. Well-fitting dresses, blouses, and skirts can be both sensual and empowering.

3. Elegant Necklines: Select necklines that highlight your collarbone or shoulders elegantly. A subtle V-neck or boat neck can add a touch of sensuality without being overly revealing.

4. Luxe Fabrics: Choose luxurious fabrics that feel great against your skin and add an air of sophistication. Silk, satin, and fine materials can enhance your style.

5. Statement Accessories: Use accessories strategically to express your sensuality. A statement necklace, a pair of elegant earrings, or a chic bracelet can add a touch of allure.

6. Play with Color: Experiment with colors that make you feel confident and vibrant. Rich, deep hues can exude sensuality while maintaining professionalism.

7. Sheer Details: Incorporate sheer elements in a tasteful way, such as sheer sleeves, overlays, or subtle panels. This adds a hint of sensuality without being too revealing.

8. Back Focus: Backless or low-back outfits can be subtly sexy. Remember to balance the exposure with appropriate coverage in other areas.

9. Heels and Shoes: Opt for stylish heels or elegant shoes that complement your outfit. They can enhance your posture and overall confidence.

10. Confidence Boosting Makeup: Makeup can be a powerful tool. Experiment with makeup styles that make you feel confident and accentuate your features.

11. Personal Fragrance: Choose a subtle and elegant fragrance that enhances your presence and leaves a memorable impression.

12. Professional Balance: Ensure that your outfits remain appropriate for the business context you're in. Balance sensuality with professionalism.

13. Storytelling Through Style: Use your fashion choices to tell your unique story as a survivor and entrepreneur. This can add depth and authenticity to your personal brand.

14. Supportive Network: Surround yourself with a supportive network that appreciates your journey and personal style. Their encouragement can boost your confidence.

Keep in mind that sensuality is about feeling comfortable in your own skin and expressing your personality. By combining sensuality with professionalism and confidence, you can create a unique and empowering personal brand that resonates with both you and your business goals. The goal is to create an image that exudes confidence, allure, and sophistication without compromising the professionalism that's crucial in the business world. It's about leaving a lasting impression through subtlety and style. Keep in mind that you will reflect your brand. Your clothing should align with your brand's values and message. Flatter Your Body Type: Understand your body type, and choose clothing that flatters your figure. Well-fitting clothes enhance your overall appearance. Pay attention to grooming and makeup that complements your overall look. A polished appearance conveys attention to detail. Have layering options like cardigans, blazers, and scarves to adapt to varying temperatures and occasions.

Fashion is a tool to enhance your brand, not overshadow it. Your clothing should complement your skills, values, and business goals, helping you make a lasting and positive impression on clients, partners, and stakeholders. You might want a Signature Piece. Develop a signature piece or style that becomes synonymous with your brand. It could be a specific accessory, color, or clothing item that sets you apart.

Dressing in a sexy and sensual manner as a female entrepreneur is a subjective choice. While personal expression is important, it's crucial to consider the context and industry norms. Here are some points to consider:

- Professionalism: The primary focus should be on maintaining professionalism. Clothing that is overly revealing or provocative might not be suitable in many business settings and could detract from the business message.

- Industry Standards: Different industries have varying dress codes. Research the norms within your industry and find a balance that aligns with your brand while still being appropriate.

- Confidence and Comfort: Feeling confident and comfortable in your attire is essential. If a sensual style empowers you and helps you exude confidence, it can positively impact your interactions and performance.

- Respect and Perception: Consider how your attire might be perceived by others. Dressing too provocatively might lead to unintended assumptions about your professionalism and priorities.

- Brand Identity: If a sensual style aligns with your brand's identity and is well-received by your target audience, it could work. However, ensure it doesn't overshadow your expertise and business acumen.

- Networking and Relationships: Building professional relationships and networking effectively are crucial for entrepreneurs. Your attire should encourage connections and conversations rather than distract from them.

- Versatility: Strive for versatility in your wardrobe. Incorporate elements of your personal style while maintaining a balance that suits different occasions.

In summary, it's possible to express your personal style as a female entrepreneur, including a sensual one, but it's essential to strike a balance between self-expression and professionalism. Being mindful of industry norms, your brand image, and the perceptions of others will help you make informed decisions about your attire.

As women entrepreneurs, you have embarked on a remarkable journey—one filled with challenges, triumphs, and endless possibilities. The fusion of your entrepreneurial spirit with a well-curated wardrobe has the power to amplify your voice, solidify your presence, and leave an indelible mark on the business world.

In your pursuit of excellence, remember that fashion is not merely about trends or aesthetics—it is a form of communication, a visual representation of your values, aspirations, and achievements. Every outfit you choose, every accessory you adorn, contributes to the tapestry of your brand identity.

As you navigate the intricate tapestry of entrepreneurship and fashion, remain true to yourself. Embrace your uniqueness, harness your confidence, and let your style become a reflection of your unwavering determination. Whether you opt for classic elegance, bold innovation, or a harmonious blend of both, let your fashion choices be a celebration of your journey and a testament to the boundless potential that lies within you.

The story of women entrepreneurs in the realm of fashion is one of empowerment, resilience, and inspiration. It is a narrative that continues to evolve, grow, and redefine the boundaries of what is possible. So, step forward with grace, purpose, and an unyielding commitment to showcasing your brilliance through every stitch, every accessory, and every ensemble you choose.

Showcase your personality and align with your business goals. Striking the right balance between style, professionalism, and self-expression will help you make a positive impact in the business world.

'Empowering Elegance' unveils the secrets of choosing the perfect ensemble, accessorizing with finesse, and navigating the delicate balance between self-expression and business professionalism.

Now go break stereotypes, shatter glass ceilings, and make a mark as a woman leader entrepreneur while embracing the transformative power of fashion. Together, we embark on a captivating journey where entrepreneurship meets elegance, where innovation and style converge, and where every outfit becomes a statement of strength, confidence, and unapologetic individuality.

May your journey through entrepreneurship and fashion be a symphony of achievement, a canvas of creativity, and a legacy of empowerment for generations to come? Here's to the women who dare to dream, who dare to lead, and who dare to embrace the transformative power of Infusing Sensuality & Empowering Elegance.'"

With utmost admiration and respect,

Dr. Maria Angelica Benavides is known as the Ultimate Legacy Builder, a well-known global publisher, visionary woman leader, networker, global traveler, international speaker, and educator. Dr. B. is now dancing and performing as one of her favorite hobbies. Dr. B is a radio host of Facturando Tu Historia and PowerTalk (Profit from Your Story) on Radio Metroplex in Arlington, Tx, the capital of sports, entertainment, and events. She is a trainer of NLP, Hypnosis, and Timeline Therapy and holds retreats around the world. As a mover, a shaker, a changemaker, and cancer survivor, she now holds Fashion Shows for women who had/have cancer to help them tap into their inner beauty, never give up, stay fearless, and be unforgettable. She believes that together we make a difference to create a bigger transformation in the world.

https://blinq.me/6XdEPTRPdsS5664TXbOl

Dr. Barbara A. Berg

How Fashion Helped Me Raise My Self Esteem - Inside and Out!

When I was a little girl, I remember my mother always trying to keep my hair cut in a very short, unattractive way, such as a

bowl cut", like just putting a cereal bowl on my head and cutting around it. I wanted long hair like my friend across the street, but she would hear none of it.

If I did or said anything that called positive attention to myself, she would say, "I love me. Who do you love?" So, one of my earliest messages to myself was to never try to draw attention to myself. However, that was never going to happen because one way or the other, I was somehow always called out front - good or bad.

The first place I do remember being allowed to stand out and feel SEEN and proud was at Girl Scout Camp. I would first wear my Girl Scout uniform and then later wear my badge sash on it, and I felt very included, supported, and proud. For the first time, I belonged! I didn't exactly call it a "fashion statement" at the time, but when I wore that uniform, I felt I could rule the world, and no one could hurt me!

Then, when I was 16, and a junior in High School, I was one of the four Angels in the school performance of the Cole Porter musical, "Anything Goes". I remember wearing a teal-colored knit pantsuit, and I felt like a million dollars!

I truly enjoyed working on that production, and when I brought my outfit home and showed my mother, I just knew she wouldn't say much about it.- However, my high school friends all liked it, and we all began dressing up more as a group and would encourage each other to wear the prettiest clothes we could get hold of and not care so much what our parents thought! (As often as we could). - Luckily, we were good role models for each other, and the black and white pictures we took of each other and the fashion statements we thought we were making meant all the difference in the world to us.

Then, I went to college in 1971. The Vietnam War was going on; the term "hippies" was a growing concept. My high school friends and I went in different directions, and I gained weight and didn't seem to "keep up" with the other girls in my dorm. While a number of my dorm mates were wearing make-up and fashionable clothes to brighten up the too long bell bottoms and sloppy blouses on top, I went the other route and went out of my way to wear no make-up and acted as if I didn't care what I looked like as long as I had long hair!

I was depressed and didn't know it. Much of the only attention I did get was for academics and getting A's and B's in school. However, deep down I knew that I wasn't being myself, and everything felt "flat" to me. What I really wanted was to be out front in the world and feel joyful and live out loud!

Finally, when I got into Grad School to become a master's degree social worker, I was asked to take an internship and teach Human Development at a University across town. I was encouraged by my incredible supportive professor, Dr. Dojelo Russell, to take great care of how I looked for my students, and I began to get into putting the best outfits together that I possibly could. Over time, my feelings toward myself and others matched the beautiful clothes I began accumulating as friends and I delighted in getting great deals in clothes wherever we could. It was such a wonderful time when we traded clothes, when we got together and felt like we were getting something brand new! We felt fashionable, and we felt we "belonged" to each other and making our way in the world.

Life started to seem as if it was coming more together for me. When I was just 5 weeks from completing Graduate School, I met the father of my daughter, and my soon-to-become husband, Ron. In meeting him, I soon met his mother, Estelle. Estelle became one of the most influential people in my life when it came to holding my head up high, sharing my love for looking my best, and fashion!

This was during the '80's when dressing up came back in, and shoulder pads were the statement of the day! Estelle was the manager of the Women's Designer Clothes Department at none other than Bullocks, located in South Coast Plaza in Costa Mesa of Orange County, California! And she was amazing! I had begun losing weight when I met Ron, but I had a few pounds to go. She never once said anything, but she would bring me clothes when she came to visit or mail them, that were just a little bit smaller or more tailored than the last time, and somehow, I always loved them and wore them with great pride and joy.

Estelle always knew just what to pick out!

After Grad School, I moved to Dallas with Ron, where we got married. He did his three years of internship and residency, and I got one of my favorite all-time jobs, Directing the First Zale Diamond Company On-Site Child Care Center from 1980-1983. Since onsite Corporate Child Care for working parents was the topic of those years, and Zale was one of the first ones to do it since World War II, I was interviewed by just about every local and large national T.V. station from around the US. Thanks to Estelle, I did the Bunny Hop with my 4-year-olds, dressed in a St. John dress. I spoke for the Governor of New Mexico's Corporate Child Care Task Force in Santa Fe, New Mexico, dressed in a Kasper Suit. I spoke with the president of Zale Diamond corporation during a T.V. interview at the Dallas Fairmont Hotel in a Calvin Klein dress, and I toured parents and visiting dignitaries through the childcare center wearing Christian Dior.

I vividly remember meeting with the FBI who "cased the place", checking it out for security reasons in case Ronald Reagan would get a chance to tour the center while he was on the campaign trail for President of the United States. I honestly can't remember the name of the designer I was wearing that day, but I walked tall inside and out, just knowing that what I was wearing was a fashion statement that fit the caliber of expression I was looking to bring out, I found myself smiling from ear to ear.

And as for my mother while I was living in Dallas working at my favorite child care center and she was living in New Jersey with my father, (whom she married and had me after she had given up her plum job after graduating Julliard, the famous school of music in New York many years ago), she sent me a professional picture that had recently been taken of her, dressed in a turquoise suit made just for her with perfect hair and make-up, as my father did "allow" her to play the organ for a national convention of County Agents of Agriculture. I was so pleased to see that she finally got her chance to be fashionable and hold her head up high! I only wished it could have happened to her sooner, and more often, so she would have had a happier and more fulfilled life and wouldn't have felt the need to take her raging angst out on me!

P.S. Much thanks to Dr. Chebra Dorsey of Ochea Fashions for including me in your first fashion show with G.S.F.E. and always supporting me in fashion, and thanks ever so much to Lady Dr. (h.c.) Robbie Motter for always being a role model for us to take pride in our fashion and show up at our best and appreciation and admiration for everyone in G.S.F.E. and those connected with our organization in some way, who support us all in feeling supported in whichever fashion of style we come to call our own!

For more information in reaching Barbara A. Berg about "Ring Shui-Move Your Rings, Change Your Life" and other books, speeches, and events, contact her at barbara@ringshui.com, barbara@barbaraberg.com, or just call or text her directly at 909-786-7201.

Dr. Elizabeth "Liz" Mezia-Celis

**Shine Bright Like a Star
&
Bring Out Your Inner Beauty**

I once read a quote by actress Celina Jaitly that said, "Fashion is a state of mind." It's also about wearing what you feel comfortable in, what you look good in, and shining your inner light and not necessarily about following the latest fashions. Regardless of how you dress and how you accessorize, the best look you can ever wear is your smile. Get up each morning, get dressed and shine your bright light like a star. Give it style, give it attitude!

I think there is beauty in everything, what 'normal' people perceive as ugly, I can usually see something of beauty in it.

— Alexander McQueen

As a photographer for more than 27 years, one of my favorite types of photography has been doing group Glamour Shot sessions. They bring a sense of playfulness and magic — a complete transformation.

"Shine bright and bring out your inner beauty" has been my motto for many years. I enjoy watching women at play while getting made up, getting their hair done, then moving into the spotlight like movie stars. As my spotlighting illuminates their glowing beauty, I allow them to dress up and choose their looks, change accessories, hats, jewelry — you name it. Everything is needed to create their glamorous look.

Together with my makeup team and our welcoming personalities, I create a space of transformation where my clients are free to be themselves. I give them a sense of ease and comfort and what comes out is confidence and smiles — the spark of their soul. They're free to express themselves, and once they sense this freedom, I can capture the true essence of their inner beauty.

It gives me tremendous joy to share that space with each of my clients. My promise to them is that they will love what they see while I inspire them, lift them up, and show them how beautiful they are.

We live in a society where there is so much judgment about what beauty should look like. Beauty comes from the inside, and it radiates outwards. There is no right or wrong. You don't have to look like a Barbie doll to feel beautiful. You wear what makes you happy and create your own style, whether you like makeup or not or you dress fashionably. It really doesn't matter. I see people's hearts and understand what they want and the image they want to convey.

Style is something each of us already has. All we need to do is find it.

—Diane Von Fürstenburg

Many people go through life carrying remnants of their wounded inner child. They have dealt with rejection, bullying, people telling them they're not pretty or good enough. Sometimes some people have to deal with an inner bully. I know I did. This inner bully, or negative self-talk, judges us for not being perfect, and it will either turn on or off our inner light. For many years, I suffered from bullying. I felt insecure about how I looked, and how I transformed those insecurities was by always following my inner desire to improve myself and never giving up.

I would watch models and movie stars getting makeovers on TV, but I would think that only those type of people could afford that kind of special beauty treatment. After finishing my associate degree in photography, I worked at a studio called Expressly Portraits where I had to learn how to give ladies makeovers. I would do their hair and make-up and then take their pictures, process them, print them, and sell them. It was a great experience because I gained so much knowledge and learned different skills. I later worked for an independent company just as a glamour photographer until I decided I was ready to start my own business.

Today, I specialize in glamour sessions that capture the essence of heart-centered entrepreneurs through visual images that create massive attention to their brand so they're able to achieve the wealth and prosperity they desire.

Our image as business owners or entrepreneurs is very important. We all want our clients to know us and have a sense of who we are and what we're about through our smiles and expressions. Remember smiles are contagious. We become a mirror that others can reflect and trust.

Smiles irradiate happiness, joy, peace, and safety. They bring out confidence, so you can be ready to conquer the world. As the owner of Photo Styles by Liz, I take pride in my core values, which create attention and change.

Beauty = Self-love

Confidence = Freedom of Expression

Peace = Essence of the spirit

Self-expansion = Transformation of self

Beauty, this is when you have reached your purpose and you just glow, radiate, smile, and your inner beauty just shines. Beauty is the mirror of the soul — an act of self-love. When we feel ourselves with love, we have so much more love to give. People will be drawn to you, feel curious, and want to meet you. The opportunities are endless.

Confidence is one of the main core values. We all need a little more confidence to take action, and this comes from feeling free to express ourselves in order to deliver our message.

Peace is one of my favorite core values. When you feel at peace, everything flows almost effortlessly and in sync with your energy. Through the essence of your spirit, you feel good and have a sense of accomplishment.

Self-expansion is an ongoing evolution that requires us to continuously improve and transform ourselves. It's our innate desire to expand our potential self-efficacy and ability to reach our goals. In other words, by believing in ourselves and in our abilities, we can complete tasks and achieve goals. The ultimate reward is that we manifest the realities within our hearts.

First and foremost, I wear what I love. That's what women have to focus on: what makes them happy and what makes them feel comfortable and beautiful. If I can have any impact, I want women to feel good about themselves and have fun with fashion.

—Michelle Obama

As a little girl my mother would always dress me and my siblings in fancy dresses and suits. We were known by our family for always being well-dressed. My baby brother was nicknamed "El abogado," which means the lawyer. He would always wear a suit and ties for parties. My mother's sisters would love to dress in fancy dresses for our family events. Fashion was very important to them. They loved wearing the latest fashion and style trends.

Elegance is not standing out but being remembered.

— Giorgio Armani

I could say I get my good taste in fashion from them. Growing up, I was a little plump but that didn't stop me. I volunteered for the Christmas play when I was in second grade. I performed and danced in a leotard and tutu to the sound of the Nutcracker. It was amazing! Whenever I listen to The Nutcracker or see plays around Christmas time, I go back in time to reminisce about my childhood memories that I dearly carry with me in my heart and soul.

One of my aunts used to sew and create her own fashion pieces. She lived with us at the time, so she would make clothes for my sisters and me. When I was in sixth grade, my school was looking for volunteers to help out for a graduation fashion show, so I raised my hand and helped them out.

Sometimes I am amazed when I think back to that moment because I was a very shy little girl. My artistic side and childhood innocence inspired me to say yes without giving it much thought. I did what I now think was unthinkable and out of my comfort zone.

But I was always an artist who loved to dress up, dance, and create. I loved to paint and draw, and I won several contests. Looking at my aunt sewing gave me the idea to make my clothes for my own dolls and later as a teenager, I began to sew my own clothes.

Through the years my creative side has helped me evolve, come out of my own shell, overcome obstacles, and shine. It has taken me to many places and opened many doors for me. For all of this and more, my heart is full of gratitude as I have been able to help others feel good about themselves through my glamour shots.

It feels great to look good, but what is most important is how you feel inside. You are the love of your life so be good to yourself and always do your best. If you obsess with perfection, it can give you many headaches. With all the love in my heart, I encourage you to always shine bright like a star and bring out your inner beauty so that you can make a difference in the world and help others shine.

People will stare. Make it worth their while.

— Harry Winston

Dr. Elizabeth "Liz" Mejia-Celis
(h.c.) Humanitarianism
Award winning photography and image expert
www.photostylesbyliz.com
Instagram: @photostylesbyliz
Facebook: Liz Mejia-Celis, Photo Styles by Liz
photostylesbyliz@gmail.com
(323) 804-0092

Heather Chee

From Wheels to Strappy Heels; Unveiling the Fashionista Within

I still recall the invigorating scent of lemon cleaner as the floors shone like an endless sheet of ice. A tall, brown-haired man meticulously finished mopping the final corner of the store. Gripping the red cart handle tightly, my mom forged ahead, maneuvering around the "caution wet floor" sign. With eager anticipation, I caught sight of the toy aisle in the distance though it still felt out of reach. A few middle-aged women complimented my outfit in passing. I responded with a shy, yet grateful smile—a gesture any young child would make towards a kind stranger. The background music caught my attention, playing a familiar tune that ignited the dancer within me. Lost in my own world, I swayed and twirled through the aisles, seeking solace in my impromptu performance. But as my thoughts carried me away, I suddenly realized my mom, now a distant figure, had made significant progress ahead. Instantly halting my dance, I hustled to catch up.

Keeping up with my mom was always challenging, especially during trips like these. They would commence smoothly, only to end in a different manner. We were approaching that critical point when my pain announced its presence, radiating from my lower back to my legs, rendering walking impossible. Tugging at my mom's arm, I confessed, "I can't walk anymore." The overwhelming pain forced me to crumple to the floor, assuming a fetal position—a routine response when the pain appeared. Yet, as the familiar agony gripped me this time, my mom and I locked eyes, knowing instinctively that this was no mere phase or game. Something wasn't right within my body, demanding urgent attention and answers.

I have vivid memories of that doctor's visit. The scratchy medical gown clinging to my skin, my sweaty palms leaving damp imprints on the examination table's paper. Seeking any kind of solace, I locked my eyes on a nearby painting —a portrayal of a doctor attentively listening to a young girl's heart. Her concerns and fears radiated through her eyes, mirroring my own emotions. I remember the room grew warmer with each passing moment, but I fought to maintain focus and composure. A loud creak followed the doctor's entrance, diverting my attention to the door. I did my best to convey my symptoms, while my mom willingly filled in the remaining details. After, the doctor paused momentarily, hastily jotting down a name on his pad.

A few weeks later, we found ourselves in another waiting room, this time at a different location, awaiting a specialist's expertise. After numerous consultations and tests, the verdict was delivered. As a three-year-old, I grappled with comprehending the weighty words: "You need surgery."

From what we were told my spine was slipping out of place, requiring a lower back fusion for stability. No amount of preparation could have prepared me for this revelation. Countless questions flooded my mind. How would the surgery unfold? Could I finally walk like other children, free from pain, running and dancing through store aisles?

It felt like a flash from getting the news of surgery and it being surgery day. I do remember awakening from the haze of anesthesia, and being greeted with the words, "Heather, your surgery was a success." Attempting to speak, my lips transformed into an exuberant smile, stretching from ear to ear. As I was wheeled out of the operating room, a gentle breeze came across my face, guiding me along the long corridor toward the room that would become my home for the following weeks.

The hospital room exuded an unwelcoming atmosphere, only broken up by a vibrant, multi-colored geometric curtain that served as a barrier between me and the other young patient in the corner. My hands clutched the plaster body cast, extending from under my armpits to just above my knees. This full-body cast was necessary to help give my vertebrae time to fuse together, forming the much-needed stability for my lower spine. It was my new reality, accompanied by a large wheelchair that aided my mobility.

As weeks bled into months, life carried on, but in a profoundly altered manner. I confronted the harsh reality of what it truly meant to be different. The stores I once strolled through on two legs now witnessed my passage on four wheels. With each revolution of the wheelchair's wheels across the polished store floors, heads would turn, gazes fixating upon me. Some would point, and though their whispered remarks may not have been intended to reach my ears, laughter would escape their lips as they muttered, "Look at her." My head would bow low, yearning more than ever for the comfort of my own home. I intimately understood the weight of being different, and I despised it.

Physically limited for six long months, during that time, something transformative occurred. My creative imagination became a refuge, an alternate reality that kept me sane. In my mind's eye, I would envision myself liberated from the confines of the wheelchair and body cast. I would dress myself in a sleek black pleather dress, mirroring the one I had seen once on TV. Completing the ensemble with striking red strappy heels. This vision portrayed a confident woman, ready to conquer the world—power emulating from her attire. In the face of challenging public moments, this fictitious version of me replayed in my mind, providing me solace and strength.

When the time finally came to part ways with my plaster body cast, an epiphany struck me. The belief I held that fashionable clothing held the key to confidence, should not be limited to my own experience. Every woman deserves to feel that same sense of empowerment. This vision transformed into my life's mission and propelled me to the concrete jungle—New York City—where I embarked on a 10-year career in fashion.

The first time my work collided with my life mission was on a Thursday evening after leaving my workplace in midtown Manhattan. I vividly remember opening the large glass doors to a noisy city crowd, but among them a middle-aged woman caught my eye. She exuded an overwhelming radiance and confidence. As she strode past me, I was drawn to the distinct floral embroidery following her left pocket. At that moment, I realized she was wearing a pair of pants I had helped develop and bring to market. Witnessing someone embrace it with such grace and confidence filled me with an indescribable sense of fulfillment. I had finally achieved my dream of providing confidence for women of the world.

These days I love wearing my pleather dress and strappy heels knowing I can conquer all that is in front of me. This confidence has spilled over into every part of my life. I have moved on from the world of fashion to the world of solopreneurship. I still believe all women should embrace their individuality, celebrate their strength, and stand tall amid the chaos through the clothes they wear. To me, being fashionable transcends the superficial, and becomes a force of liberation, empowerment, and self-expression. To me, fashion possesses a profound transformative essence, an extension of the inner power that resides within everyone.

Dr. Angela Covany

The Essence of Fashion and A Wardrobe's Influence

Each of us possesses a natural flair for creativity and expression, which we channel through our unique sense of fashion. Clothing is more than just a covering; it is your canvas, your voice, and your armor against the world. I believe the right outfit can not only make you feel confident but also allow you to stand out in the sea of artistic brilliance. As we browse through our closets, we see that each garment was a chapter of our life, tied to a memory. I occasionally donate any garment associated with negative experiences to keep my outlook positive. I encourage you to do the same. I have learned that clothing is not just about aesthetics, but about communicating your story, values, and aspirations. Your wardrobe is an extension of your identity, a means to connect with others on a profound level. The clothes you wear are more than just garments - they are a reflection of your journey and an invitation for the world to join in weaving the grand design of human connection. What we wear sets the tone for how we feel about ourselves, shows the world how we are feeling about ourselves and reflects much more than we realize. It is important for us to make a conscious choice on how we choose to dress and present ourselves to the world around us.

I was taught as a young teen a few very valuable lessons in life by my amazing mother. Those lessons were as follows. There is a time and a place for everything. Dark make-up should be worn at night or for special occasions. Make-up should be minimal to enhance the natural beauty that was given by God. Dress respectively and to dress in fashions that fit my personality. I was encouraged to always be myself and never feel pressured by the latest fashions or to feel pressured to have to dress to fit in.

My Eighth-grade graduation was an informal celebration with a dance that followed. I will never forget. Upon arrival, one of my classmates showed up in the same dress. The entire night everyone was joking about my twin. I had tried to not stand out with my clothing in an attempt to just fit in the entire year. I occasionally wore my hair in beehive updo but that was the extreme of me letting my unique style out. My freshman year, I truly took these lessons in and decided to wear attire that no one else was wearing from different time eras to show my uniqueness. What I didn't realize at the time was that I was attracting more people to me than away from me. I remember thinking, I want to attract friends that like me for who I am not what I am wearing. I wanted to make genuine friends and genuine connections. I did just that and still have many friends from my high school years.

Over the years, I have remained comfortable dressing in what I like without the restraints of worrying if others will like it or discuss it later. I have learned that inner beauty is far more important. How you treat others, how you make others feel, and your character is more important where true beauty is concerned.

Dr. Chebra Dorsey

Growing Up with Fashion

As an African American kid growing up in San Diego, California, in the 1960s, I didn't have a lot, but I had enough. I remember getting dressed up for church on Sundays and Easter to attend church service at Philadelphia Baptist Church. Boy, that was fashion at its finest for me wearing sheer overlays made of pink and blue lace, flowing dresses with ruffles, lace anklet socks, and my beautiful shiny strap shoes. Wow! Talk about sharp. It was Sunday's best, and everywhere you looked men and women wore gorgeous hats, and the men donned their finest suits. Back then, laying out my clothes to wear, I remember if everything didn't match, it wasn't the proper attire, and your look wasn't put together. Times have really changed with today's mix and match "anything goes" attitude. Never in a million years as a young girl did I dream I would grow up to become an award-winning celebrity fashion designer, CEO of Ochea Fashion Productions. God works in mysterious ways.

As I became a teenager, my awareness changed, I would see stunning pinstripe suits on men and exquisite tailored dresses full of flowers on women, but as I looked closer, something was missing. I became aware that even though they looked fabulous on the outside, I felt negative emotions pouring out of them from the inside. I remember thinking to myself, "How could someone look so beautiful on the outside and seem to be so unhappy or negative on the inside?" Don't get me wrong, I wasn't perfect, but I couldn't help noticing that what was on the inside was reflecting on the outside, and shouldn't we want to portray a balance between both sides when striving to look perfect? After years of investigating this topic, I've concluded that many play it well under the guise that the more you dress up, the more you cover up, but this didn't sit well with me, I wanted to lift the veil. So, I've set out to change people's perspective by focusing on the inside to get their hearts and spirit in the right place first with the help of fashion. I've created What Are You Wearing? The Inspirational Spiritual Side of Fashion.

As this amazing concept began to take root in me, I found myself contemplating what are people really wearing when they put on that fancy expensive name brand outfit or that tacky poor fitting unsophisticated dress? What about when they chose to wear a camouflage print pantsuit with army boots over a 60s bell-bottom flared one? I began to question, "Are they actually wearing what they're wearing to glow outwardly?" I didn't think so from what I saw, and many times what I saw made me feel danger! Don't get me wrong, I found there are those who mean well even if all they were doing was pretending to look at the sparkle on the outside. Then again, there are those who have a purpose. Yes, I said a purpose, a purpose to be the best of who they really are, not just someone hurting so badly on the inside no light can shine on the outside.

I remember growing up, nothing mattered but the light of God, and it was what all of us were seeking, and what all of us should still be seeking today. It wasn't high fashion or your Sunday's best outfit; it was who you were as a person in the eyes of God. You wouldn't have to dress it up to cover up negative emotions and sin; your light would shine perfectly from the inside, and you would sparkle on the outside touching the hearts of everyone you met. All people around the world love fashion from top designers, and they spend thousands yearly combing major department stores or thrift shops for designer names to create their unique wardrobes. Unfortunately, millions are dressing themselves to cover up the pain, loss, heartbreak, abuses, or failure in their lives instead of finding out God is on the inside, and they should be dressing themselves from the inside first.

I've helped thousands of women look and feel fantastic in my boutique and online store by focusing on helping them to let their inner light shine. The way I do it is by talking to them about their relationship with God to get them to focus on everything he's brought them through. I help strengthen their faith by teaching them to let go of past hurts and pain and remember how much God loves them. Each of us deserves to love ourselves as God loves us to find our true radiance. This is the key to finding personal style through beauty, fashion, body image, hair, makeup, jewelry, even press on nails. It's so rewarding to me to see the before and aftereffects of my client's transformations when they dress themselves from the inside first, and you should see them smile. It's a package deal for me when it comes to fashion. I feel beautiful and grateful thanks to God shimmering inside of me, and I get unsurmountable joy telling somebody else they are as pretty as a picture now, and everyone who sees their smile will be caressed by God's presence inside of them. What are you wearing?

Have you ever noticed when you go to a fashion show or watch one on TV, the famous designers have all the supermodels lined up dressed to the nines, and most of the time, each model has the same haughty attitude with no smile on her face as she struts her stuff down the runway?

You are the Fashion

Yes, for that show it's all that, but after the lights and fashion do you feel the same or whatever you wore made your life great? Imagine loving your garment. Wow that outfit becomes more beautiful. Fashion is temporary when it comes to you. Did you know you are the fashion first before the garment? You see, fashion doesn't make you; you make the fashion by feeling good and letting go.

When I design, I like color because I was always shy of color. We are miracles of light like a mirror. You see yourself in the image, but you can't see the inside. Being beautiful on the inside is a fashion statement for yourself like mothering yourself, loving yourself, and being confident. I know that having these three things can start your fashion off right because you feel like color or something that looks and feels fabulous on you.

I believe spiritual fashion should come first to reflect the fashion you are wearing. I would see a person with just a basic dress, nothing fancy, but her inner light shined through, and she looked even more beautiful. What is it that she's reflecting from the inside? If you feel fabulous you should look even more fabulous. That is what's important.

It's very important to know who you are as a person first, because it reflects off of you. Did you know that you are the fashion? Yes! How you represent yourself is fashionable. How you carry yourself is fashionable. How you act is fashionable. There are so many things that fashion plays in your life like your character or your persona. Is your fashion going to help somebody, or is it going to bless somebody? Yes, we're still talking about fashion. Or are you a true fashion icon with a statement to encourage or to set a great example in someone's life. Yes, I'm still talking about fashion.

Did you know that clothing is not in control, but you are? You are clothed in God's majesty. You are the fashion for our future. What you represent to others makes a big difference in other people's lives. Fashion is what you feel, and how you give impressions to others. Start from the inside then represent to the outside.

Color is you. Flowers are you. Prints are you. It's rich and personal to you, and we're here to give that richness to others. Yes, this is fashion. You are the key to somebody else's fashion. You are clothed in riches. Fashion should just enhance what you are. Each of us is giving a fashion show every day, and we are designed by God, fashionably made to help one another. Yes, fashion is very important. You are the nation of fashion, and what you give from the inside is the purpose for fashion. Yes, you are clothed in what you give, dressed already in God's attire. Yes, those days are going to come when you don't feel as if you are clothed in richness, but even whatever you put on, you are still clothed in God's garments. It's not what you're wearing; it's what you're feeling that makes the garment stand out. Colors are you. You are the designer. The design is you. You are a one-of-a-kind design.

A Purpose to Design through Fashion

Yes, you are flashing who you are in front of everyone's eyes who see you through your fashion choices. What are you going to represent to somebody else? What are you going to inspire through your designs in somebody else? You need to ask yourself what moods and colors are you going to give them? What style dress or suit are you going to flaunt your stuff in? You'll never go wrong if you always design from your heart.

That way you'll always be wearing what you want to give them. That's what fashion is. You are on the runway of life each day. Are you ready to showcase what you've designed for yourself to the world? Each of us is beautiful. Each of us is stunning. Each of us is one of a kind. We all have a purpose to fulfill our highest potential in the eyes of God, and fashion is a wonderful way to start expressing yourself. For example, maybe color is you, or maybe you're "I'm independent", so find a starting point, and design your layers of fashion from there. Keep telling yourself, I'm here to represent fashion that has a purpose for my life so where should I start. Look for ways for your fashion statements to make a positive influence to lift other people's spirits.

There are so many ways to design and so many different designs in life to choose from. Some people have darkness in their designs, and that's what they want to wear. Remember darkness already had light from the beginning, and more light that was added by God and his son Jesus Christ to make the world a more beautiful place. By adding color to your soul inside first with the word of God, your fashion can emanate a lighter state of being, and you can become more fashionably exquisite and glowing.

We all have designed darkness at one time or another in our lives while relishing in it and feeling comfortable in it, but light in God's image is always available to us, and it changes darkness by the way it's fashioned or designed. It's how you represent it in relation to your purpose to love a style for good intention and motivation. It's not the dark color that matters. It's you! You can change it at will. By prioritizing your life, you can change your fashion to represent a higher elevation of your soul.

Always design for your style as you sew or pick out your garment. Always design showing yourself in the image you want people to see you in. For example, ask yourself questions like, do you want your style to be confident, classy, bold, or simple for each occasion you're dressing for? Make sure when you're finished designing your garment or look that you're happy with it because pleasing yourself and being comfortable in your own skin is what matters most. Does your finished design represent the stage of your life you'll be walking on? Do you need more color or prints before you hit the runway? Are you ready for people to see who you really are?

I wonder how many people can put themselves together by choosing their garments to portray love, compassion, peace, joy, forgiveness, passion, faith, kindness, inspiration, hope, caring, power, even mentoring. Your choices should highlight what you are all about, a one-of-a-kind queen or king with royalty. I bet that's the most powerful dress you could put on. Imagine showing yourself in your highest spiritual light displaying to the world your soul's elevation from the inside radiating vibrantly on the outside.

Being stylish should always be changing for the better so that you're ready to help others with your style in case it's your style they're looking for also. When you stitch your garment or take time picking it out, you need to take time and design a new you that's always evolving and always changing. You should never just throw something together. Each layer and accessory should be draped in a special, unique, loving, and caring way, your goal being to make yourself stand out beautifully. By taking time to build a new you each time you get dressed, you'll obtain the wow factor where all eyes will be on your stunning garment on the outside beaming because of what you are on the inside. You're the fashion!

Customizing Your Garment

Many times, and as the years go on, we'll probably want to add something to our garments or change our style. I like to call this customizing your garment to go with the changes in your life or public trends that might appeal to you. Life is all about change, and your own personal style will change along with it. We can't let becoming too comfortable with the same style or let fear of what other people might say stop us from experimenting with new looks and colors that might take us to greater heights hold us back. By keeping your mind open to customizing your garment to create a new you, you will always be recycling items in your wardrobe and never feel outdated. If you have a new outlook on life, it can become a breath of fresh air to incorporate it into your new style and the garments you choose.

Your fashion is unique, it's one of a kind, and nobody can take it from you. It's yours for you to represent yourself and your connection to God from the inside out in a beautiful way. Style yourself in an uplifting way, the way you want to put yourself together to feel special. What do you want to portray to others? Cherish your decisions and stand behind your choices, because your one-of-a-kind look can bless someone else and bless yourself and that's what makes your original style and the way you carry yourself special.

The Industry of You

Did you know that the fashion industry and the apparel and textile sectors are the 4th largest in the world? The fashion industry has a huge impact on the economy and has a major contribution to the global economy. The industry plays a fundamental role in social cultural life with a global workforce of 3.4 billion people involved in fashion, clothing, and textile production. It employs approximately 430 million people, and fashion entrepreneurs act as the wheels of the fashion industry. They push the fashion industry forward through design, innovation, and new business models. Everyday hour of every day the fashion industry is there to help you find yourself through fashion and develop your own personal style. Wow! That's why it's a billion-dollar industry. People are putting themselves together whether they realize it or not.

To some, fashion might be healing by wearing loose-fitting clothes, to others it might be to get more attention or stand out, and to others it might be a personal career expression like an artist choosing to wear a bright colored smock. To another person it might be just to showcase a major change in yourself to your family, friends, or coworkers. The reasons behind your personal choices go on and on and that's why there are millions of fashion avenues available for each of us to explore. Fashion doesn't make you; you make the fashion, so be fashionably you.

A Passion for Fashion

When you have a passion for fashion, it's all about putting your best into everything you want to design for yourself. You need to believe in your heart, fuel your desires, and find the passion you must have to influence others in the right way. Passion is the key to not giving up on believing in yourself and what you're capable of creating to show the best of you. You have the power within yourself to bring your passion and love forth to the highest degree until you feel it completely and can express it through your style and choices.

I can't stress enough how important it is to express your passion for your garment in a humble way. So, take your time and be patient; your passion garment is a structure only you can build. Make sure your garment fits properly, is the made of the finest material you can afford, and it displays the colors or print pattern you want for the exact moment you'll be wearing it so you can step out and have your inner light shine.

Building Your Colorful Enlightenment

Your beauty on the inside plays an important role in your life for what you portray on the outside. Color is one of the most important choices you can make when designing an outfit? So, let's build something exquisite as you think in terms of how certain colors make you feel when you see them and clothe your body in them. Think about how you really feel when you wear red, or blue, or purple, and all the shades in between. The color of your garment plays an important part in how you feel when you put on that color, so choosing the right color can make a difference between success or failure and influence your mood tremendously. At all times your color choices must come from the inside because you'll reflect the color you're giving out to the world.

To start with, see the color you have in your mind's eye because you might not be wearing it. If you're not wearing it, you might feel off because you're reflecting the wrong color, and this in turn can influence the people you meet if they also perceive your color choice is off. Spend time meditating on what color/s you'd like to wear for a certain event. Visualize them in your mind's eye. Spend time wrapping yourself in different colors and patterns as you look at yourself in the mirror. Your eye will tell you what colors and prints go best with your complexion and hair color etc. Expand your vision to think outside the box like, What's the color of life for me? What's the color of love for me? It's your spirit that makes the garment beautiful, light, and right for you, not the other way around.

Hemming Your Dress

Sometimes things seem as if they will take forever when all they really take is time. It's good practice to exercise patience when you're hemming your dress because you have come so far seeking adventures and conquering obstacles, but it benefits you to finish your garment. The purpose being to see it through to completion to reap the rewards, but you can't do it without patience. When you're in the final stages of sewing your garment or finishing up a shopping spree, you enter the no worry stage because everything finally comes together for you.

Hemming your own garment is a lot of hard work because you must be very careful and precise, trying not to go out of the lines to keep your stitching lines even and make it look flawless and finished. Some people may find it tedious, but with practice you can learn to enjoy this special time putting the final touch on your garment or store-bought item. None of us are perfect, but each of us is trying to look perfect. By exercising patience while hemming you'll learn to take the time needed to make the chore of completing your garment a beautiful and rewarding experience. It's a wonderful time to have a fixed purpose, a time to think, a time to love, and a time to understand that its time used wisely as apply the finishing touches of love and beauty for your garment to sparkle and reach your highest expectations upon completion.

Once finished, step back, look at it, and relish how far you've come, and how beautiful you are in your one-of-a-kind design and style. Yes, you're not perfect, but you're evolving and striving to have nothing wrong with the state of perfection you find yourself in. Imagine how your inner light will shine out from the inside as you step out in more than just style, you'll be stepping out emanating the light of God and your gratitude from within, and you'll look gorgeous on the outside everywhere you go. Your garment is now beautiful and original like you.

Get Ready for Your Fashion Show

Now get ready for your fashion show, ready, set, go! It's time to show the world who you are and what you've created through your style and garment choices. Yes, you, your light, and your choices come together. People are waiting to see you come alive in a new light through your style and garment choices. So, stand strong with love, patience, and beauty as you proudly display who you are on the inside and how you feel. Now's the time to showcase your purpose for life freely in front of the world without inhibition because you are a child of God. Your passions and everything that's special about you should shine through each outfit and the way you carry yourself down to the smallest accessory.

You're a masterpiece. You're a creator. You're a beautiful messenger that's here to build others up, not compare yourself to others or compete with them. You're your own unique commodity. You can smile and hold your head high knowing you're a child of God, and that you've created something of value that no one can take away from you. God created you in all his glory. What's for you is in his divine plan for you to receive, no one else, and there's nothing for you to fear.

I'm so proud to have you as a beautiful visionary for fashion where your choice in one garment could have the power to take over all the world where people will be saying, "Wow! I want that. I need that. She or he really took the time needed to showcase something beautiful." Just look at what you made on your own runway displaying your soul and life. A standing ovation to beautiful you!

Time to Price Your Garment

Well, the fashion show was a hit, and now people want to know what's the price. Either what it cost for you to make it yourself or the cost you paid to purchase each item. Jesus paid the price for us, and now it's your turn. Sit down and recall all you've done including the sweet memories of your garment, the love you put into it, the time and passion, the pain you felt and talked about, the colors, the power, your time, and patience. It's all there, and now it's time to price your garment. I'll give you a secret; the prize is you. You are the one standing up and approved to show the world the glory of who you really are. A masterpiece of favor in God's eyes. It's your garment, and you know inside if your price is too high or too low. You're the one who put it together in a state of thankfulness, you have no price, but your garment does. You're now a standing art of luxury and brilliance. Congratulations on the garment of you.

As you read all the chapters on fashion and are inspired by my select group of authors in the book, remember that you're a garment of beauty and art who's now destined to become a change maker for the world. Thanks be to God.

Dr. Virginia Earl

The Essence of Fashion
Fads Are Fads; Classics Are Timeless

Fashion is not just keeping up with what's in style. It's a language that externalizes the essence of who we are without using words. It's the mirror image of our inner-self — how we feel, who we are, and how the world sees us during a certain period of time and place. It's a form of self-expression, freedom, and individualism reflected through clothes, footwear, accessories, make-up, hairstyle, perfume, shapes, colors, lifestyle, and spirituality. When we wear clothes, we like and love, it boosts our confidence and helps us stay focused.

Social Identifiers as Fashion Statements

Create your own style… let it be unique for yourself and

yet identifiable to others.

— Anna Wintour —

When we select the clothes, make-up, and accessories we want to wear, whether it's a day-to-day choice or a special event, we send subliminal messages about who we are to the world and what "tribe" or "group" we identify with. We show off who we are to the world by the brand names (or lack thereof) that we wear, which are normally identified initially by colors, shapes, and styles.

Some of the elements that may affect our behavior and self-confidence are color, comfort, fit and style. Fashion also describes our inner character, mood, sexuality, and social status. We use clothes to make a fashion statement and attract the situations and people we want to surround ourselves with during different stages in our lives.

Although at first glance we may not consciously place each group's style in separate categories, we are able to identify their differences. Some of the categories may include the business or power player look, minimalist, classic, busy mom, street pack, artsy, intellectual, creative, or statement makers, such as bohemian, preppy, exotic, French, and the list goes on.

A Mood Shifter

Elegance is when the inside is as beautiful as the outside.
— Coco Chanel —

How we feel from the moment we wake up determines the tone we set for the rest of the day. There are times when we might feel morose, so we have no choice but to put on our best clothes in the hopes that looking superlative will give the world the impression that everything is fine when it's not.

There's a lot of truth in what we wear projecting how we feel internally, but there's more to it than that. I see fashion as a mask to hide how we truly feel and uplift ourselves, as well as raise our spiritual vibration and reduce our anxiety and other negative emotions. Dressing up soothes us by counteracting negative energy that we create or absorb from others. Sometimes disruptions in our lives will lead us to abrupt changes in style that can be manifested in different ways, marking the end of one stage and the beginning of another. We do this by either completely changing our hairstyle and/or our overall look. It's almost like a rebirth celebration of our soul.

In this sense, clothes play an important part in our lives because they alter our mood almost immediately. Whatever it is we're feeling at any particular moment, negative energy will have a ripple effect on those closest to us. However, when we make a conscientious effort to shift our mood by wearing our favorite clothes, make-up, and perfume, our energy immediately shifts to a higher vibration, producing a positive effect on ourselves and others.

Using Color and Emotions as Guides

Everyone has their own style.

When you have found it, you should stick to it.

— Audrey Hepburn —

What we wear is often triggered by our emotions, which subconsciously guide us from the deepest part of our soul to pick those colors and styles that reflect how we feel at that point in time. For example, we might be asked to follow a certain dress code when we are attending a particular event. This might include certain colors and styles conforming to a specific theme.

It's through color that we project low and high vibrations. All colors, including black and white, have their own spiritual meaning. For instance, violet has the highest frequency and the most energy. It is spiritually associated with peace, independence, wisdom, creativity, devotion, power, ambition, sensitivity, spirituality, luxury, wealth, and more. Violet motivates, inspires, uplifts, and balances. So, ladies, if these are some of the elements you want to attract, wear more violet!

In contrast, black and white are not considered colors. Black, in particular, is considered a shade, and in its own absence of light has no specific wavelength. Neither does white, as it contains the summation of all colors.

On a personal level, regardless of the color's own spiritual or physical meaning, each color produces a different effect similar to how perfume triggers positive or negative memories stored in our subconscious. Knowing whether a color, perfume, or other element might trigger happiness or sadness will make a huge difference when we're in the process of deciding what to wear.

Following the Latest and Greatest

What you wear is how you present yourself to the world, especially today, when human contact is so quick. Fashion is instant language.

— Miuccia Prada —

Just because something is in style, it doesn't mean you have to wear it. The latest fashions don't necessarily look great on everyone. Hence, when we place more importance on wearing the latest style instead of what compliments our physical features — our natural beauty — like the biological lines and shapes of our face and body, we lose the essence of our own style and an opportunity to present our personality and unique creativity to others. When something is forced, it never feels or looks right, and we end up losing ourselves in a trend that might not necessarily convey who we are.

I am well aware of what will and will not look good on me. For this reason, I don't force the latest and greatest fashion upon myself just to look trendy. When the distressed denim look came out, I refused to buy a pair of jeans with holes because I didn't want to look like everyone else. Fads are fads; they will always be replaced by new ones.

Everything has a time and place. It's a great thing to be unique and stand out from the crowd, but it's also a good thing to do it with class and style without losing your inner beauty — your essence — that resides in the inner depths of your soul. It's the one thing that will always distinguish you from everyone else, and that's uniquely YOU.

The beauty of a woman is not in the clothes she wears, the figure that she carries, or the way she combs her hair. The beauty of a woman is seen in her eyes because that is the doorway to her heart, the place where love resides. True beauty in a woman is reflected in her soul. It's the caring that she lovingly gives, the passion that she shows and

the beauty of a woman only grows with passing years.

— Audrey Hepburn —

——

Fashion is the essence of our soul that we

willingly externalize to share who we are with the world.

— Dr. Virginia Earl —

Virginia was awarded an honorary doctoral degree in humanitarianism from GIA in London, and she's a best-selling author, speaker, editor, writing coach and spiritual healer living in Southern California. She may be contacted via her Facebook handle "Virginia Earl Editor" or by visiting www.sevenmysticrings.com, www.translationsunlimitedsa.com, and www.virginiaearl.com

Marneen Fields

Fashion is an Expression of Dexterity for Talent to Shine

I'm honored to be contributing a chapter to fashion designer Dr. Chebra Dorsey of Ochea Fashion Productions' book What are You Wearing? The Inspirational Spiritual Side of Fashion. I became fascinated with Chebra's unique spiritual concept for the book and was thrilled when she asked me to also write a chapter.

As one of Hollywood's most prominent pioneering stuntwomen of the 70s and 80s (as Wikipedia lists me), I chose to tailor my chapter towards what has inspired me most about fashion throughout my career as a famous stunt actress. For me, fashion has always been an avenue that's enabled me to express my great physical dexterity and talent even before my years as a stuntwoman starting with my years as a competitive champion gymnast performing and practicing in multi-color leotards and stretchy stirrup sweatpants with bold stripes. I'll share some wonderful stories about much work on some films and primetime TV shows shortly, but first I'd like to take you back to the beginning and how my mom and sports helped me create my own personal style.

My personal, overall, go-to lifetime style that's stood the test of time and where I still hover towards today for overall comfort and freedom in fashion comes from stretchy form fitting fabrics like polyester, rayon, lycra, silk, spandex, and the lightest cotton because they feel best on my skin. I wouldn't have achieved what I've achieved without my fashion choices being somewhat of a second skin on my body allowing me absolute freedom of movement with the lightest additional weight.

My beautiful mother, Ruby Marie Farris-Fields' style, was sheer perfection. She was 5'6 ¾" tall, slender, immaculate, and gorgeous. All items in her wardrobe were starched and ironed flawlessly; she even pressed front seams into my brother's Levis. Ruby's long fingernails were always exquisitely manicured by her, and her bleached dyed back hair ratted high in the ultimate 60s style. She loved wearing Marilyn Monroe pedal pusher slacks and a white button up cotton blouse with matching white tennis shoes with white peds that had a pom pom outside the heel of the shoe or no socks. Lipstick was her go-to makeup item, and she always looked clean, cool, and miraculously put together. I never saw her look tacky or sloppy, and I always felt like a geeky short 5'4" Tomboy athlete next to her. My dad, Robert Leo Fields II, was just as spotless and well-dressed as she was; his shoes were always shined, and his hands and nails were always scrubbed with a brush he kept at the kitchen sink. They both took great pride in their appearances and instilled it in me and my two brothers. However, I'm a cry short of their scrupulous painstaking, and one of my brothers has disregarded it altogether.

Growing up, my mom took me shopping at Sears for all my school clothes. She loved to tell stories about how she dressed me in adorable lace and fluffy petticoat dresses as a toddler with little black patent leather shoes and thin white lace bobby socks. I have many photos of me dressed as an adorable little princess thanks to my beautiful mother. My mom was a feminine lady, and she was determined I'd be one, too, and thanks to her I am. I still remember the day she bought me my first pair of 1" high heels. She spent hours teaching me how to curl my hair with sponge rollers, how to file, buff, and polish my fingernails, and how to make sure my bras fit properly when I got old enough to wear one. She was also my hairdresser and groomer. I love her so much recalling these special memories of how she took the time to help me with my grooming and fashion. I was always sitting in a chair in the middle of the kitchen while she trimmed my bangs and hair and plucked my eyebrows. I trusted her taste in what she thought looked best on me even when she wanted me to wear hot pants in high school to show off my showgirl legs. Because of Ruby, I sit up straight, suck my belly in so I don't look like a mountain goat, position my legs a certain way in photos so I photograph flattering, and hold my head up high with good posture when I walk.

I remember one horrific fashion disaster that's left me vulnerable and self-conscious to this day. I was in 7th or 8th grade and got invited to attend a party at a restaurant with my friends from Culver City Jr. High School. I was so excited to get the invite and combed my closet for the perfect outfit. I found what I thought would be terrific to wear to the party, a pair of light olive-green pants (tight like today's leggings) with a slight bell bottom flair at the bottom over a pair of my 1" high heels and a flowery blouse. I waltzed into the party with my head held high to see I was what's called "under dressed," being the only young lady who wasn't wearing a dress or skirt. I shrank in embarrassment to low levels of devastation as everyone gave me funny looks and others made comments like, "Why are you wearing those pants?"

My only rebuttal was, "Hey, I love these pants."

To this day, the sexiest thing a man can whisper in my ear is, "I've bought you a dress; go try it on for me; it's laying on the bed."

"Yes, Sir!"

I promised to share with you some stories about what fashion was like for me as a Hollywood stuntwoman stepping into the shoes of 100 of the most famous actresses in the world of the 70s and 80s to perform death defying stunts for them and for myself when I was cast in a role and performed my own stunts. Back then as a pioneering stuntwoman specializing in high falls, high dives, prat falls, and fight scenes, I wore a little boy's football girdle, knee pads, and thick elbow pads under most of the clothing I had to perform in. When performing stunts for other actresses I never saw the clothing I'd be wearing over the pads until the day of the filming; fittings were almost never available for the stunt doubles. A wardrobe designer would go shopping and pick out the wardrobe for the actors to wear, and she'd pick up other various sizes for the stunt doubles like a 6, 8, or 10 if the actress was a size 6 to make sure it fit the stunt double. I was also always put in a wig, so my hair matched the hairstyle and color of the actress I'd be performing stunts for. When I doubled Jayne Seymour on Battlestar Galactica, I wore a long brown wig that was to die for, and, believe me, it got me lots of attention and cat calls walking around the Universal Studios lot.

So right off the bat you can see how hard it would be to perform in clothing you've never worn with all the pads underneath along with wearing long or thick and curly cumbersome wigs and foreign jewelry. Sometimes, I wasn't able to wear the pads because my actress was wearing shorts or a spaghetti strap dress. My shoes also had to match the shoes the actress was wearing along with any jewelry. I beat up Stacy Keach in an episode of The New Mike Hammer doing a karate fight scene in high heels. I jumped (feet first) 72 stories high off the First Interstate Bank building in downtown Los Angeles before it burnt down wearing a long sheer robe, matching negligee, a pair of fluffy slippers with gold pointy heels, and a thick curly wig for the TV series Quincy. You can see why I've titled my chapter "Fashion is an Expression of Dexterity and Talent to Shine," because for me it was.

I remember the day I arrived on the set of The Fall Guy to double one of the most beautiful women in the world, Priscilla Presley. The wardrobe designer handed me a pop art dress made from the finest silk my hands have ever touched. As she handed me the dress and told me the name of the famous designer who designed it, she also added, "Don't rip it during your stunt." So now I'm not only concentrating on doing my stunt in the gorgeous dress of fine silk, but now I must add to the forefront of my mind the distracting comment of, "Don't rip it!" Another time I was at the top of Catalina Island performing stunts running through a dirt field with explosions going off around me doubling Michelle Phillips of the Mama's and the Papa's for the film The Man with Bogart's Face. The wardrobe designer handed me a very tight pair of white jeans to wear and a blue blazer, and she told me, "Don't get the jeans dirty!" The blazer was taken off Michelle for me to wear, and when I reached into the pocket, it had the butt of a marijuana joint in it. So now two worries as I'm performing the stunts, "Am I getting the pants dirty? OMG, there's a joint in the pocket!"

The first thing you learn when becoming a pioneering Hollywood stuntwoman coming from the arena of being a champion college gymnast tumbling on mats is the mats are gone. You now need to perform these death-defying feats onto the payment, gravel, sand, breakaway tables, and more. You learn very quickly you not only have to follow seemingly impossible directions from the director or stunt coordinator to nail your stunt in one take as I was known for, but you also must follow outside directions from the wardrobe designers, props department, lighting techs, cinematographers, special effects, and other stunt people who might be in your scene. However, I wouldn't have changed any of the situations I found myself in and the mind-blowing experiences I've had as a result of them because the challenges of application of exquisite dexterity through the avenue of my physical talents was the ultimate reward of expression like nothing else for my spirit to shine in this lifetime.

Marneen Fields Bio: Marneen is an award-winning WGA registered scriptwriter, ASCAP composer, SAG actress/former Hollywood stuntwoman, best-selling international author, and a pop-blues/soft rock adult contemporary artist. She's appeared in 150 films, primetime TV shows, web series, music videos, and theatrical productions since 1976. She's worked with famous A-list directors, actors, and producers like Clint Eastwood, Stanley Kramer, Irwin Allen, Priscilla Presley, Tom Jones, James Garner, Shirley Jones, Michael Caine, Jeff Goldblum, Dick Van Dyke, and many more. Wikipedia lists her as one of the most prominent stuntwomen of the 70s and 80s, once coined Hollywood's Original Fall Girl. Today, she's the CEO and creative director of Heavenly Waterfall Productions. She's making her directorial debut this year with her award-winning screenplay *Who's Gonna Take Care of Me?* A trued drama about saving a mentally ill and homeless mother. She's a 5-Star rated author on Amazon for her, *The Illusive Craft of Acting: An Actor's Preparation Process.* Her autobiography, *Cartwheels & Halos: The True Marneen Lynne Fields Story* is being published summer of 2024 by TBNs Trilogy Publishing who has a two billion audience. Her filmography,

Rolling with the Punches with a Hollywood Fall Girl has been picked up by Briton Publishing and will be published worldwide in the summer of 2023. She's one of the featured authors in *The 100 Most Inspirational Women in the World* publishing soon. To date she has won or been nominated for sixty-five awards in film and music competitions around the world for her screenplays, music compositions, acting, singing, and stunt work. She's been interviewed on over 200 TV/radio shows, and for magazine/newspaper articles circling the globe. Marneen spends her time traveling from Las Vegas to Los Angeles for live performances, acting roles, and speaking engagements.

For more, please see her IMDB page at,
http://www.imdb.me/marneenfields

Monika Schaible Photography

Ada Gartenmann

Designing a Sustainable and Fashionable World: Empowerment Through Style

Introduction

Clothing has the power to transform how we feel about ourselves, providing confidence, security, and even a source of amusement when faced with outdated perspectives. For me, fashion has always played a significant role in developing my leadership and is an integral part of my life. In this article, I will discuss the importance of sustainable fashion, the power of colors in our wardrobe, and how fashion can be a tool for self-expression and empowerment.

The Power of Fashion in Challenging Times

Women often reinvent themselves during challenging times, such as after an emotional breakdown, changing cities, or jobs. Following fashion trends shouldn't be limited to wealthy women; it's a way to boost self-esteem and showcase our personalities. It also brings people with similar tastes together, creating conversations and bonding experiences.

According to a study by Pine and Gilmore (1998), experiences can become a source of personal growth and self-improvement, which can be applied to fashion-related experiences.

Sustainable Fashion in the Post-Covid World

In the post-Covid world, transformational leadership that turns vulnerability into strength is essential. During Women's Month, let's celebrate the women who lead and support each other's successes. I couldn't ignore fashion during the global Covid crisis, so I organized a sustainable virtual congress that brought together women from all over the world. We discussed new trends, the future of fashion, and how major brands made their money.

Sustainable fashion has gained significant momentum in recent years. According to a report by McKinsey & Company (2020), more consumers are prioritizing sustainability and ethical practices when purchasing clothes. The Ellen MacArthur Foundation (2017) also highlights the importance of transitioning to a circular economy in the fashion industry to reduce waste and pollution.

The Power of Colors in Fashion

Colors can influence our self-esteem, energy, and even success at social events. They play a crucial role in personal image, conveying emotions and empowering our appearance. For example, according to a study by Labrecque and Milne (2012), blue symbolizes authority and control while black represents elegance and luxury. Green is associated with nature and sustainability, white with purity and neatness, and yellow with happiness and positivity. Finally, red embodies power and passion.

Fashion as a Tool for Self-Expression and Empowerment

Fashion is not just for the wealthy; it's an opportunity to express yourself, make connections, and open doors for new conversations. Think about where, why, and for whom your money goes when you make a purchase. Over the past decade, fashion has been linked to over-consumption, environmental pollution, and labor exploitation (Joy et al., 2012). Sustainable fashion aims to end poverty, promote fair wages, and use eco-friendly manufacturing processes. Ultimately, fashion is about self-expression and empowering your feminine leadership.

Conclusion

Embracing sustainable fashion, understanding the power of colors, and using fashion as a tool for self-expression and empowerment not only enhance our personal lives but also contribute positively to society and the environment. By making conscious choices and supporting ethical practices in the fashion industry, we can create a more sustainable and equitable world.

As an advocate for sustainable fashion, I encourage people to educate themselves on the environmental and social impact of their clothing choices. By supporting eco-friendly brands, participating in clothing swaps, and shopping second-hand, we can reduce waste and pollution while still enjoying the benefits of fashion.

Overall, fashion can be a powerful tool for self-expression, personal growth, and leadership. By embracing sustainable practices and understanding the impact of our choices, we can create a positive change in the fashion industry and beyond. Let's work together to design a more sustainable and fashionable world for all.

As the CEO and founder of SIMA Global Foundation, a bestselling author, mentor, and motivational consultant, I strive to be a true inspiration and role model to many around the world. By embracing sustainable fashion, understanding the power of colors and using fashion as a tool for self-expression and empowerment, we can make a positive impact on ourselves, our communities, and the environment.

"Fashion---it's our expression of the way we our leading."
- Ada Gartenmann

References:

1. Ellen MacArthur Foundation. (2017). A new textiles economy: Redesigning fashion's future. Retrieved from https://www.ellenmacarthurfoundation.org/publications/a-new-textiles-economy-redesigning-fashions-future

2. Joy, A., Sherry Jr., J. F., Venkatesh, A., Wang, J., & Chan, R. (2012). Fast fashion, sustainability, and the ethical appeal of luxury brands. Fashion Theory, 16(3), 273-295. Retrieved from https://www.tandfonline.com/doi/abs/10.2752/175174112X13340749707123

3. Labrecque, L. I., & Milne, G. R. (2012). Exciting red and competent blue: The importance of color in marketing. Journal of the Academy of Marketing Science, 40(5), 711-727. Retrieved from https://link.springer.com/article/10.1007/s11747-010-0245-y

4. McKinsey & Company. (2020). Fashion on climate: How the fashion industry can urgently act to reduce its greenhouse gas emissions. Retrieved from https://www.mckinsey.com/~/media/McKinsey/Industries/Retail/Our%20Insights/Fashion%20on%20climate/Fashion-on-climate-How-the-fashion-industry-can-urgently-act-to-reduce-its-greenhouse-gas-emissions.pdf

5. Pine, B. J., & Gilmore, J. H. (1998). Welcome to the experience economy. Harvard Business Review, 76(4), 97-105. Retrieved from https://hbr.org/1998/07/welcome-to-the-experience-economy

Ada Gartenmann is the CEO and founder of SIMA Global Foundation, a bestselling author, mentor, and motivational consultant. With over 25 years of experience in fashion, beauty, wellness consulting, and lifestyle expertise, Ada is a multi-award-winning social entrepreneur

and humanitarian. She has received numerous awards and accolades, including the U.S. Presidential Lifetime Achievement Award and the BAFTA Diversity Award. Ada is passionate about providing equal opportunities through education and leadership, focusing on single mothers and child survivors of domestic violence living in extreme poverty. As a bestselling author, mentor, philanthropist, and business consultant, Ada strives to be a true inspiration and role model to many around the world.

Pat Jinter

A Fashionable Reflection

I say dress to feel good. Your style should be worn with an attitude of Gratitude. Therefore, whatever enhances your divinity is a fashionable style. It's all about experience, and if you feel good, you will look good in whatever makes you feel good. It has nothing to do with being a puppet for anyone; it's all about feeling good about who you are and letting that attitude of gratitude show in every step you take. Now that's a fashion statement. Feeling good is the new fashion that's wearable and can go anywhere and enter into any space.

Style really is on the person; it can be a way to distance yourself from yourself through the latest styles and colors which can be evolving from certain trends that appear over and over on the street or the runways.

Fashion reflects who you are and how you feel at a given moment, reflecting your personality, character, mood, and style revealing your true identity. Fashion is a way of life for some, more of a hobby or interest than forms expressions of oneself. Being able to use it how you want, each individual decides what he/she chooses to do with it. Each decides his/her own taste and destiny for whether a trend, craze, style, the latest stage whether chic or by enthusiasm.

Fashion truly is a way to express yourself to others. Anyone who tells you, it doesn't matter what you look like to others is badly mistaken. It really does matter as the way of dressing well unlocks doors both personally and in professional life. Fashion is a way to empower yourself and influence others as it is constantly changing.

Be inspired to be your own person and wear whatever you want and dress up with your own choice of jewelry, handbags, and footwear.

It's impossible to be bored in the fashion world as you may be as creative as you can be pushing the limits and boundaries through one's own confidence.

People judge another in seconds so explain through the dress of fashion who you are. What you believe is who you truly are!

Hope you got what needs to be gotten because you know I can get deep. I am not in with the norm. I think it's abnormal to be like everyone else when you are unique. When you develop an attitude of Gratitude for yourself, whatever you wear is fashionable.

Sending love and light. ♥

Pat Ginter

Independent Thrive Brand Promoter

go.thrive.go@gmail.com

Ph: 1-306-551-9236

Regina, Sk. Canada

Kristie Jacobo

Rock the Feminine Fashion in a Man's Profession

Picture this, the sun is coming up on a beautiful spring morning in San Diego, CA. It is 6:00 AM and I have arrived at the job site. My morning task as a gas pipeline Project Manager is to walk the job, meet with the contractors, and set the parameters for the scope of work for the construction team. This is not the typical job setting for most women. Gender roles have historically placed women far from the construction industry. The penetration of women into the construction industry is rattling cages, and I am here to tell you, we can look good, too!

I have learned that the fundamental driver to success in a male dominant industry is feeling confident in how I carry myself. As a woman, I want to feel good about how I look. To be a boss, I must feel like a boss. Like most job settings, there is a dress code. When I am out in the field on a job site, I must wear boots, long pants, safety glasses, a hard hat, and yes even the dreaded orange vest. Ladies, these items were not designed to make us feel sexy. Construction workwear caters toward men. Workwear companies responded to women entering the construction industry by shrinking the men's clothing and adding a more feminine color pallet. Body shape and feminine curves were not considered. The result is oversized clothing such as a boxy style shirt or a work vest that is getting caught above the belt because the size of a woman's hips is not factored. So, what is a girl to do?

Women are expressive. We like creativity. We pay attention to detail. When I walk out the door, I might check all the boxes on the dress code list, but then I add my feminine twist. I am wearing rhinestone studs in my ears. My hair is curled. My lipstick is on point. With little room to accessorize, I add a variety of funky and fresh glasses of all colors and shapes. My nails glitter. My belt buckles accentuate. Show up on site and find me wearing my hot pink polo shirt or a polka dot blouse under my fireproof jacket. To take it a step further, I might even wear a lacy bodysuit and matching panties. These elements are not visible, but I know I have them on, and I feel confident.

Take a few more steps with me, and you'll enter my changing room, also known as my car. After all, I might have an important meeting following my site walk. Being prepared with a versatile wardrobe and a few clutch items is essential. In my car you will find a blazer to replace my jacket and a pair of leopard print flats or heels to replace my work boots. "Hat hair" has kicked in, so I am equipped with hair bands, berets, or a scarf. I'm not promoting extravagance, just a few simple tips to share my fashion.

What does fashion mean to me? It means wearing my confidence to break barriers without compromising how I look or feel. It means a handful of lipstick shades and a few versatile pieces, and I can conquer the day. I hope to see more women with boots on the ground in the construction industry. I want young women to look forward to a career path as a Project Manager or a Construction Manager and know that they can get the job done and still sparkle on the runway, even if it's a desert path.

Dr. Cherilyn Cee

**"From Hidden Scars to Runway Stars:
Fashion's Transformative Power Embracing Dignity"**

The clothes we put on every day tell a story and communicate to the world who we are, as well as significantly impacting our emotions and spirit. Growing up, I had many illnesses, including excruciating eczema, asthma, and allergies. During the spring and summer, the pollen in the air triggered more reactions. I dreaded summers because the heat accelerated my sweating, causing unbearable itching and making my cracked, dried skin rub inside the creases of my legs, ankles, feet, arms, neck, and face.

After intensely scratching, I was left with weepy sores, scars, and discoloration. When my mother made me wear stockings, the infection from the sores oozed through them, gluing the fabric to my legs. Peeling them off was excruciating, trying not to rip my skin. Sweltering days caused the sores to produce a disgusting odor that stunk up the classroom, making me a perfect target for bullying.

Kids in elementary school singled me out, throwing rocks and dirt at me because the skin around my eyes, mouth, and neck was rough, dry, peeling, dark, and scaly. They thought I looked and smelled this way from not bathing and poor hygiene. I was terrified to go to school. I made sure I was the last student to arrive and the last to leave to avoid the kids tormenting me, calling me names like "Black Tar Baby" or "Lizard Girl."

My legs were almost amputated at seven because the oozing bloody sores were misdiagnosed as a flesh-eating disease. I promised God if he saved my legs, I would become a healer and help as many people as possible. Right before the scheduled surgery, a compassionate doctor refused to amputate and formulated a solution to heal the infection.

I was alone 98% of the time, feeling abandoned. The emotional and physical scars left me with very little self-esteem, and I had a hard time speaking with people. I was confined to my bedroom, where I played with paper dolls, designing their adorable little outfits.

It's ironic because my unique fashion style broke the ice with the kids at school and had strangers asking me, "What are you wearing?" Ultimately, fashion boosted my self-confidence, altering the trajectory of my life and allowing me to fulfill all of my dreams, including becoming a healer.

My mother was the ultimate homemaker. Each meal was a sacred celebration, bringing us together for prayer, reflection, and gratitude. Even though we were very poor, I did not feel it as a child.

My mother shopped for us in thrift stores because we didn't have money for new clothes. Everything in our wardrobe was recycled, except she bought our socks and underwear. She washed the second-hand clothes, took them apart, redesigned them, sewed them, starched and pressed them, making them look brand new. I studied how she converted ordinary items on the rack into stunning pieces of art.

In grade school, I wore dark garments with long sleeves and pants to cover my skin, even in summer with sizzling heat. People would do a double take when they saw how I was dressed and ask, "What are you wearing?" I remember my friend Kit asking, "What are you wearing? She said I dressed like a little old lady.

In the eighth grade, I was happy going to school because I could take home economics. Sewing class played a crucial role in my life. I began creating interesting silhouettes and exciting shapes that flattered my body, so it wasn't obvious that my patterns were intended to cover my body. I was learning to choose astonishing textiles with more vibrant colors to uplift my mood.

The ninth grade was a pivotal time for me because I started wearing my designs to school. I was still ashamed of how my legs looked. Therefore, I made various hip-hugger pantsuits. Shockingly, my creative outlet profoundly influenced my classmates and changed their impressions of me. They began noticing my inventive approach to fashion and started treating me differently.

My mother was very strict and forced us to dress conservatively, not allowing us to wear tops cut too low, showing cleavage or the belly button. I discovered a clever way to block the view of my stomach, creating one of my signature blouses—flowing fringe dangling underneath the bra line to cover the mid-drift area.

I vividly remember attending the Greek Theatre wearing a white suit and blouse with orange fringe flaring out like flames from the sun. I was stopped multiple times, "Where did you get that? What are you wearing? Your outfit is extraordinary!" I began enjoying public events and meeting new people.

In high school, my one-of-a-kind designs helped me come out of my shell and create friendships. My new friends and I decided to enter the high school talent show as the singing group the Supremes. I made all our costumes. The scars on my body were not as pronounced, so I showed my legs for the first time in our matching fluorescent blue micro mini dresses that shimmered with sequences and won the contest. My mom didn't see those dresses or other revealing clothes I made. I became an expert at changing my clothes on the way to school or elsewhere.

Fashion is what saved me! As time went on, I became more social, learning to love myself. I ran for student body secretary and won. The accolades began because my love for fashion made me stand out, changing how others perceived me.

In high school, I was asked to join the modeling troop Great Time Fashion (GTF), which put on fashion shows. I was tall and thin and loved my 4-inch heels, making me appear taller. I have modeled at influential banquets, benefits, and events from Beverly Hills to South Central. GTF allowed me to model some of my own personal designs along with the clothing from the stores.

Before I was married at 19, I started attending the local Junior College, where I continued to wear my own creations. I was well known for my fashion statements, so much so that I ended up in the school newspaper several times.

While in college, my English instructor wanted me to be in a beauty contest. I thought he had lost his mind, but he said it would help me develop my personality. Reluctantly, I committed to being in the Thai International Beauty Contest even though I was swamped working full-time while attending school. I modeled an exquisite sleeveless long white satin evening gown I designed, exposing my arms.

My friend from Thailand won the competition. To my surprise, I was first runner-up, then we both stood on stage together. That was the first time I was in front of a crowd without people making fun of me. Allowing people to see my flesh opened me up, helping me evolve into the person I have become today.

My mother made our clothes because our income was low. Watching her methods and shortcuts helped me later in life enjoy making many of my three beautiful daughter's clothes, even though I could afford brand-new ones, as I founded my own Holistic Healthcare Clinic and my non-profit, the Nu Wellness Development Foundation (NWDF), keeping my promise to God to be a blessing to others. NWDF provides free screenings and healthcare services to the disadvantaged, especially the most vulnerable, like the elderly, disabled, minorities, and those who suffer from chronic illness.

For Church on Sunday, every Saturday, I made myself and my three daughters matching outfits that coordinated with my ex-husband's suit and tie so the entire family had a new ensemble. Each week, I also made tiny darling bows out of the matching fabric to go in my daughter's thick luscious hair. I ensured we looked like the picture-perfect family even though he stayed out all night, cheating on me most of the week. After healing more of my trauma, I developed inner strength and resolved to end the marriage.

After my divorce, I was continuously invited to many extravagant events. I didn't have the time to do my hair after working long days, so I created accessories that looked like crowns, which quickly clipped into my hair. First, I took newspapers and shaped them to form on my head. Then I covered the newspaper with fabric or rhinestones in several colors to match my outfits.

Some people thought I was full of myself, acting like a queen since I wore a crown. By this stage in my life, I had overcome my insecurities about people judging me and dressed to make my soul sing without concern for others' opinions.

Along with crowns, I designed fascinators and hats to match my outfits. My passion for hats came from my grandma. My favorite black and white polka dot hat is a nod to her. I've embellished everything, including my shoes, by adding buttons from my jacket or using bows, pearls, sequences, or notions.

One night, someone was on their way to pick me up. I was in such a hurry, making a pantsuit, that I literally sewed the needle into my finger. I pulled the needle out of my hand, bandaged it, and finished the suit. Then I wore my new creation out that same night and had a fabulous time.

Several decades later, I still design most of my wardrobe, although I hire incredible women to sew them for me since my time is focused on helping those less fortunate with critical health conditions. Throughout my 71 years, I have had a chance to understand human behavior, including how fashion affects my emotions, self-esteem, and identity. Although I wore primarily dark colors in my younger days, now I appreciate bright, lively, cheerful colors because I know they will put a smile on my face and lift me up before I walk out the door.

Through the years, I've been able to express my personality through my choices of garments and accessories. In my youth, people gasped and asked, "What are you wearing because they were shocked and horrified by the awful heavy clothes that did not fit the season. No one could figure out why I would wear such inappropriate attire. Nowadays, when people ask me what are you wearing, it is because my designs are like poetry in motion turning heads for all the right reasons.

Fashion has been the glue that held me together throughout the years. I didn't have to try to become something or someone else to make others like me. Fashion helped unleash my authentic self. Every stitch I made was like taking a small step toward my destiny. I flourished in my own way as I weaved the fabric of my life together. Not only did fashion give me extraordinary fundamental self-confidence, but it also took me on a glorious journey toward my true and highest potential.

Without fashion helping me to heal the emotional scars and transforming my self-esteem, I would not have achieved the multitude of awards and recognition from government branches at every level, from the US State Department to the Los Angeles City Council, including four United States Presidential Lifetime Achievement Awards from President Obama, President Trump, and President Biden. I also received the 2019 HerStory Award for my audiobook "Written Before I Was Born" from the International Women's Federation for World Peace USA, where I serve as an Ambassador.

Sara Cypps

FASHION 101

Fashion should be fun. I love to express my inner self through how I dress and have fun in the process. I'm a 70's girl who appreciates things that are handmade and extremely unique. You name it: tie dye, lace, bell bottoms, print with some extra print on the side, fringe, washable silk; enjoy playing with different fabrics and textures. Now, ladies, let's definitely go for comfort, but for me it's all about making a fashion statement with shoes. Sandals, mules, wedges, heels, boots, or sassy flip flops make an expression with your feet but make sure you do it in style as well as comfort. We all have our favorite shoes that we can last 3-4 hours in, and that's it! So always have a spare cute and comfy pair that you can switch into if your event goes long, or your feet simply give out mid-way through. Besides, after the first hour or two no one is looking at your feet, especially if you're sitting, so be kind to your lower extremities. Overall, enjoy experimenting with different colors, textures, and fabric combinations to express your inner fashion diva.

A Accessorize. Turning a simple outfit into something with much more pizzaz can easily be done by properly accessorizing. Add a chunky necklace, a few bracelets, a ring or two, and some fun earrings, and watch your outfit come alive. Finishing your style off with a signature hat is always a fun touch, especially if you're attending an outdoor event. I recently was at a ladies' tea that was held outdoors and out of the 60 attendees; half of them were wearing hats. The hats not only complimented their lovely outfits but kept the sun out of their eyes and off their faces, which helps us to stay more youthful. Also, belts are a really cool way to dress up or to finish off your look while accentuating your waistline drawing attention to the smallest part, your waist. So have fun with accessories and express your inner princess; she loves to see you sparkle.

S Show off your assets. Often ladies are embarrassed or even slightly ashamed of certain parts of their bodies. Ladies… you are perfect just the way you are. We're meant to have curves, so let's embrace them. However, my rule of thumb is less is more. Don't wear tight pants and a tight T-shirt! Do wear tight pants and a flowing blouse or loose pants and a tight top. Unless you're in a yoga class, you don't need to have all tightly fitted clothing! The exception to that rule is if it's an evening gown, but still then it doesn't need to be skintight; a little flow high or low is perfectly acceptable. When it comes to showing off your arms a little, please be kind to yourself. A summer dress with a spaghetti strap can easily be layered with a lightweight scarf or sheer wrap that not only covers most of your arms but also gives the look a little something extra. Also, a top or dress with a cold shoulder is a great compromise; you can show off your arms and let them breathe while feeling less vulnerable in that department. So, ladies when showing off your assets, be expressive, be comfortable, and be classy.

Hair and makeup. Depending on the event or situation you may need to dial it back or turn up the heat. When you're going to a black-tie event, or similar, then bring it with class. As far as your hair goes, experiment with different styles and keep your look fresh. Whether you're wearing a wig or sporting your natural locks, change things up a little every now and then. For example, an updo is always a great look and will especially help keep your body cooler in the summer months and is very elegant with evening attire. However, keep in mind, if you're doing a photo shoot or performing on a live stage, then you will need twice as much makeup as you think you would and a little hair spray to keep your look on point. If you're working with a makeup artist, trust that they know what they are doing. It may seem like a lot looking at yourself in front of the mirror, but the camera will love you. On the extreme opposite, if you are going to the pool for a few hours, then don't forget your waterproof mascara to doll up your lashes and a little shimmer gloss on your lips. Other than that, when you're outdoors, just make sure you use a good 30 SPF sunscreen to protect your beautiful face and help keep you moisturized. Remember, most mineral powder makeup has a 30 SPF so if you're going to a backyard barbeque or casual event, you can still look fabulous and protect your skin without looking as if you're over doing it. Whatever the event, use good judgement in your hair and makeup choices, take appropriate action for the type of gathering, and have fun experimenting with different styles and colors.

Integrate old and new. Some styles come and go, but others are simply timeless. Hold on to a few of those vintage pieces in your closet and pair them with new items. For example, a beaded top or old denim jacket or jeans rarely ever goes out of style. Denim fades and gets softer over time, so the more it's been worn and washed over the years, the better. So why not embrace that old denim piece and add some bedazzle such as a little sparkle or new fun buttons. You can give them a little update yourself or find a local dry cleaner that has a seamstress on duty to help get the job done and bring your vintage clothing back to life very inexpensively. Also, if you're up for thrift store shopping, usually you can find one or two signature pieces that were rarely or ever worn. Finding a hidden treasure second hand is a fabulous way to add funky and fun to your wardrobe without breaking the bank.

Own your style. I've had people on several occasions stop me on the street because of something amazing I was wearing. Whether I bought items as an outfit or just pieced them together from different vendors and different times… you know when it's a showstopper. However, "Owning your Style" is also a frame of mind. When you know you look good, you feel good, even if you didn't feel that way before you got dressed that day. Some days our outsides don't match our insides and vice versa, but if you're feeling a little low, a cute outfit can help lift your spirits.

Never apologize for being yourself. Every woman should have the right to express herself through dressing in a manner that directly reflects their inner beauty. Fun and flirty floral prints, business attire, bathing suits, sports suits, lingerie, you name it. You be you, and don't let anyone tell you otherwise. Hold your head up high and know you are beautifully and wonderfully made and have the power to light up any room you walk into, no matter what you're wearing.

Amb. Cady Dr. Robbie Motter

Fashion is a Booster for one's Morale

I have always loved dressing up. I guess it's because when I was young growing up in Foster Homes, I never had that much of an opportunity, but as I got older, I felt great when I planned what I was going to wear.

My fashion style depends on what I am doing that day. I remember when Covid hit. I stayed in Pajamas for two days and found myself depressed as I had no makeup on and no jewelry and so I said to myself "snap out of this and get yourself dressed". What a difference it made!

Fashion is many things to me, and I love dressing up. I look at my calendar every day to see what the day's activities for me are and dress accordingly except if I am going to a formal event I will not put on a formal dress in the morning, but every day I find something to wear. It could be a dress or pantsuit or long casual dress; then I must have the shoes and purse to match so I pull that out. The next step is looking at the jewelry and getting it all together. Then I get dressed, do my makeup, and feel as if I can take on the day.

I dress up in makeup and jewelry even if I have no big plans to go anywhere. Maybe it's just a visit to the local 99 cent store. I always feel great, and I get so many compliments from people who say to me "You look great, love your jewelry, love your dress etc.." It is such a nice feeling to have those kind words from complete strangers.

It does not cost a lot of money to be dressed. I get 90% of my things at thrift shops, so because I do not spend a lot, I can have more of a selection of clothes. I even get gowns that I wear to galas from thrift shops. I have not been in a department store for years and years as I know exactly where the right shops are for me. When I walk in, I look for color to catch my eye. I pull it out to see if it's my size. I never try on things as I feel if it does not fit me, it will fit one of my members, and a few times that is exactly what has happened. I also find great shoes and purses in thrift shops and coats, so I am able to have quite a selection of clothes.

Over the years I have learned that I look best in tailored straight type dresses--not full ---and there are some colors that do not work for me.

I remember the days in 1980 to 1985 when I worked in New York, and we would go to the theatre in gowns and men in suits. Now I understand they even show up in shorts. The same goes for church. Before people showed up really dressed nicely with hats even, and now the only time I see that is Easter to show off their Easter outfits or Christmas. The rest of the time it's very casual. Also, people do not dress up when they fly anymore. I always dress up as one never knows who you might meet when you show up. The first view is you and how you look.

Many of my GSFE sisters are like me; they like dressing up and do and feel good when they do. I dress for me; I don't care if I show up and I am the only one in a long casual dress and everyone else is in jeans. That is my style that fits me. I wear jeans sometimes, but most of the time my pants are dressier with tops.

I also love wearing hats and got away from it for a while. I remember one time at an event someone came up to me and said I did not recognize you without your hat. Also, once I was at Chicago airport going up an escalator, and this guy was going down on the other side and looked at me. When I got to the bottom, he said to me, "I love women who wear hats, and I saw you. and you looked stunning and just had to tell you."

I love seeing men in suits. California seems too casual to me, but when one goes back east, we can still see the man in his suit and tie which to me looks great.

When I went to the Academy Awards for years, I always loved seeing all the gowns that the actresses wore, and I think when I started going to the Emmy's and the Awards was when I started adding gowns to my wardrobe.

I have only a few designer things that I have gotten from Celebrity designer "Ochea" who is doing this book. She knows my style, so those items reflect me. I have never owned an expensive purse or shoes as I can find shoes that look good on me that don't cost an arm and a leg. I think even if I had tons of money, I still would shop the way I do and take the money to help others rather than spending it for things that really are not a need or want.

Material things don't make us happy. What I think is a better way to be happy is to reach out and touch a life and make a difference. Those people you help don't care if you are wearing designer clothes and purses and shoes; they look at your heart and know that because of you their life is being changed.

I can't imagine why people would spend hundreds of dollars for torn jeans that I really don't think look that great. I think of how many families that money could feed, and I can wear a perfectly nice pair of jeans from the thrift shop that maybe cost me under $10.00. Plus, every time I buy something from a thrift store that money goes back to help someone. That touches my heart.

We recently did a clothing swap where many of my GSFE members cleaned out their closets of clothes, purses, shoes and hats that they no longer wear. We had close to 100 bags of clothes come in on the day of the swap. Members came and looked at all the clothes we sorted on racks and tables and the shoes, purses, and jewelry, and it was such a fun afternoon. We had food, too, so it also was a great networking time, and individuals went home with some great stuff and were thrilled. We still had 30 bags left over that we donated to one of our members for her Vet women's group, so that was a win-win day of fun, networking, and also doing service to others. This event was done by our Young Ladies GSFE group, so they, too, were learning about giving back. This is our second year of doing this, and we will do it again next year.

Recently one of my daughters was moving, and she had tons of clothes, shoes, and stuff and she gave me 6 bags of great stuff for the clothing swap and during the move she found 6 more bags of things, so I brought the stuff to my house and called some of our members that were size 8 to 10 her size and size 9 shoes. It turned out that 11 members benefited from her donation. They also had fun trying on things and leaving with some things. In two days all the stuff was given out, and everyone was happy. My daughter was happy that others would be enjoying her things---some she had never worn. My members are all sizes and all shapes, and all have different styles and colors they like so I never have trouble when things are given to me as I know exactly where they need to go, and it's FREE.

I do meet people occasionally that say, "They would never wear clothes others have worn" and that is their choice, but I think they miss out as they could be missing some great treasures. Many that say that though are willing to donate items so that is great also.

Ochea the designer has such a great eye for design that when she designs something, she knows exactly what color and what style you look good in and designs things with her clients in mind. She herself always looks like a fashion plate and always gets stopped on how beautiful she looks. People feel good when they wear her clothes as they know that she made them specifically with love and care for their style to make them look fabulous. Everyone I know that has bought one thing from her loves it, and many have graced magazine covers all over the world wearing the House of OCHEA designs.

So, what is your fashion? Be yourself. Dress for YOU---not what others are wearing. You should feel when you put on anything, how fabulous you look because you deserve it as you are fabulous so step out and step up and dress up every day and see what a difference it can make as people see you and say, "WOW! You look terrific in that color, that style, etc."

Check out thrift stores near you; one of my favorites is Angel View, and I love a church store also in Fallbrook, CA. I always find just the right things not only for me but some of my members as well. I pay attention to what looks great on my members, what colors are great for them and when I see something, I say, "WOW, this would look good on and have the person's name in my head." When I give it to them, they love it, and maybe I have spent way under $10.00 for the item. One day in the church store all the dresses were $4.00 each. We had already spread the word to members about the store so before our monthly Fallbrook GSFE meeting, you can see them in that store looking for their special thing as well. I never feel bad when I wear something that someone else has owned. I am grateful they donated it to the thrift store so I can have it or share it and then later can donate it for another person to love it and enjoy it.

Designer expensive things for some is what they must have and that is okay. I know who I am so I do not need to wear them to impress anyone. I would rather use my money to make a difference, but that is my choice and may not be yours, but one never knows maybe if you step out and see what the thrift shops have in your area, you just might say "there is some great stuff here, and when I buy it, I am helping a great cause."

One of my members Dawn Schultz started a project many years ago. At first it was called Operation Prom Girl, and now it's the dresses and dream project. She started it because when she was in High School, she could not go to Prom because her family did not have the money to buy a gown, and later in life she had a daughter and she was divorced and found out that could happen that her daughter could not go so she reached out and had gowns and shoes and jewelry donated and asked girls who needed them to come and try them on and pick what they liked for free. Over the years this program has grown, and each year because of her dream hundreds of high school girls and military women vets get gowns and accessories free and are able to attend their dance and/or prom. These young girls and women vets don't care that someone else owned them. They are thrilled that they get to pick a gown so they can go to their event. Over the years bridal shops have also donated new gowns to this project. So, think of all the young girls' lives she has touched, and each year that number grows.

One of my members who works at home was not dressing, and she saw me dressing all the time. She decided to start, and she told me, "You are right. One does feel better, and it makes me even work better as I feel so good about myself." So, take time and find out what fashion really means to you. Read the stories in this book as I am sure you will be inspired, and once you start doing it you will feel fabulous.

* *

Lady Dr. h.c. Robbie Motter is the founder CEO of the Global Society for Female Entrepreneurs (GSFE) a 501 c3 nonprofit global network. She is also an award-winning author, International Speaker, and an event planner. Her mission is to help women learn the power of SHOWING UP and ASKING which will help them soar higher than even they imagined.

Her websites are robbiemotter.com, globalsocietyforfemaleentrepreneurs.org She is on Facebook and LinkedIn as Robbie Motter. Her email is rmotter@aol.com

Dr. Jaya Sajnani

Fashion as the Radiance of Inner Beauty and Smiles

Fashion has long been synonymous with beauty, style, and self-expression. In the ever-changing world of technology, fashion has emerged as a powerful means of communication and self-discovery. To many, fashion is more than just a superficial art form; it embodies the essence of inner beauty and serves as an inseparable part of their identity.

Fashion, a mesmerizing art form, weaves together the threads of self-expression, creativity, and identity. To each individual, it resonates differently, sparking a unique emotional connection that transcends the mere cloth and fabric. For me, fashion is akin to the radiance of inner beauty and the warmth of a smile—elements I cherish and wear with unwavering dedication, no matter what each day brings. The relationship between fashion and smiles goes beyond just physical appearance. It is about how fashion influences emotions and mental well-being. When someone wears an outfit that resonates with her personality, it boosts her mood, enhances her self-esteem, and helps her feel more at ease in social situations. The joy she experiences from this alignment is evident in her smile.

Fashion stands as a beacon of authenticity, beckoning us to embrace our true selves. It allows us to paint the canvas of our bodies with colors, textures, and styles that mirror the hues of our souls. When I delve into my wardrobe, I find not just clothes, but a collection of memories, aspirations, and emotions encapsulated in each garment. Fashion philosophy lies in the belief that true beauty emanates from within. It is a radiant glow that emanates from a heart's content and a spirit at peace. Just as the smile on my lips reflects the joy within, my fashion choices mirror the happiness, confidence, and love I hold for myself. Each outfit becomes a celebration of my uniqueness, a testament to the acceptance of my flaws, and an embrace of my strengths.

At its core, fashion is an extension of the human spirit, a canvas upon which we paint our unique narratives. The clothes we choose to don and the accessories we adorn ourselves with reflect our deepest desires, values, and emotions. It is a language understood by all, transcending barriers of language and culture, allowing us to connect with others on an intimate level without uttering a single word. For some, fashion may be seen as fleeting trends and fleeting fads, but for others, it is a sanctuary of authenticity. Like a protective shell, it envelopes them, providing comfort, confidence, and a sense of belonging. As I navigate through the tapestry of life, fashion becomes my trusted companion, ever ready to uplift my spirits. On days when the sun shines brightly, I might opt for vibrant hues and bold patterns, mirroring the exuberance in my heart. Conversely, on days when clouds loom above, I might choose softer tones and comfortable fabrics, cocooning myself in a warm embrace of serenity.

In recent years, the fashion industry has witnessed a significant shift towards inclusivity and body positivity. Designers, brands, and influencers are embracing models of diverse shapes, sizes, and ethnicities, reflecting a more realistic portrayal of beauty. The role of fashion extends beyond individual expression; it has the potential to drive positive change on a global scale. Sustainable and ethical fashion practices are gaining momentum, promoting environmental consciousness and social responsibility. When individuals choose to support brands that prioritize sustainability and fair labor practices, they contribute to a brighter future for the planet and the people who inhabit it. This conscious effort to make a difference can be seen in the genuine smiles of those who know that their choices align with their values.

Fashion is not without its challenges, however. The pressure to keep up with ever-changing trends, societal expectations, and the influence of social media can lead to self-doubt and a sense of inadequacy. This pressure may push some to conform to trends that do not resonate with their true selves, dampening the radiance of their inner beauty and smiles.

To combat these challenges, it is essential to foster a culture of self-acceptance and self-love. Fashion should be viewed as a tool to enhance individuality rather than a means to seek validation from others. By encouraging a mindset that celebrates diversity and uniqueness, we can empower people to find their authentic style and embrace the beauty that lies within.

Ultimately, the connection between fashion and inner beauty transcends the superficial allure of clothing. It represents an intimate relationship with oneself, a reflection of the ever-evolving journey towards self-discovery and self-acceptance. Just as the snail's shell grows with it, these individuals embrace the evolution of their fashion choices as they grow and transform along life's winding path.

Inner beauty, often described as the glow that emanates from a soul content and at peace, finds a tangible expression through fashion. The garments we choose, the colors we select, and the accessories we cherish are not just a superficial façade; they are an outward manifestation of the beauty that resides within. To them, fashion is not an empty vessel to be filled with the latest trends but a mirror reflecting their true essence.

Life, with its myriad challenges and surprises, can sometimes throw us off balance. But fashion, like a suit of armor, stands ready to bolster our resilience and fortitude. The smile I wear becomes a symbol of courage and hope, a gentle reminder to find joy even in the face of adversity.

Through fashion, I embrace the strength to face the world head-on, with a heart full of optimism.

Fashion, to me, is not confined to a realm of trends or societal standards. Instead, it becomes an art form through which I narrate my story to the world. It whispers tales of growth, self-discovery, and metamorphosis as I evolve with each passing day. Like an artist refining their masterpiece, I experiment, blend styles, and create my fashion tableau, revealing the depths of my soul.

In the pursuit of fashion that embodies inner beauty and smiles, I often find myself drawn to the little details—the delicate embroidery, the handcrafted jewelry, the textures that delight the senses. Each element carries a story, a connection to artisans who pour their passion into their craft, mirroring the passion I infuse into my own life journey.

In conclusion, fashion, to me, is an expression of inner beauty and the effervescent joy encapsulated in a smile. It is a language through which I communicate with the world, narrating tales of self-acceptance, resilience, and optimism. My fashion choices, like a kaleidoscope, reflect the hues of my emotions, capturing the essence of my ever-evolving identity. Embracing fashion as a celebration of my true self, I wear my inner beauty and smile with pride, no matter what the days bring forth. By embracing individuality and celebrating uniqueness, fashion becomes a powerful tool to spread joy, positivity, and self-acceptance. As the fashion industry continues to evolve, it is crucial to promote inclusivity, sustainability, and a mindset of self-love, ensuring that fashion remains a beacon of radiance and smiles for generations to come.

Let's connect.
Dr. Jaya Sajnani
Entrepreneur Philanthropist, Author, Public Speaker
Founder/CEO of YG Travel, and Helping Hand Foundation
Board Director and UK Chairperson of LOANI Global
Advisory Board Member - 100 Successful Women in Business, GTC, USA
Global Ambassador, BMCC, City University of New York
Web: Www. ygtravel.co.uk
E: jayasajnani@yahoo.com
WhatsApp: +447808 522157

Dr. Charmaine Summers

Fashion Statement

I feel when I dress up, I am representing who I am and how I feel. Growing up I went to Catholic School, I had to wear a Kelly-green plaid jumper dress from kindergarten to 4th grade. Then grades 5-8 I wore the same Kelly-green plaid colors but now a pleated skirt with a white oxford button up white blouse and I loved it. Finally, I was off to a Catholic High School, Mater Dei. I couldn't wait as our uniform had more choices pink, powder blue, and red for summertime. In the winter, we had a choice of a gray plaid skirt or a red plaid skirt. Wow, I was so excited to have these wonderful choices of what I knew as fashion at that time. I was able to wear matching ribbons in my hair as well as some shoe changes, not always black and white saddle shoes. I loved my new choices of uniforms and was proud to wear them. We also had what was known as a free dress day where everyone was allowed to wear street clothes to school. I remember my sweet mother Lucy would take my siblings and me shopping, and we would be able to choose an outfit to buy for free dress day.

Now the pressure was on as wearing a uniform was always safe. Now I had to fit in with the right choices of fashion; it was as if now I felt the judgement of my peers. Yikes! Fashion was always who you hung around with as well as fitting in. I always tried to look my best.

Later in my college years, there were no more uniforms. I realized I had to create a style. I already had done this in the past years as I was an athlete, and so I dressed sporty and being a golfer at a young age, I had already leaned toward argyle sweaters and polo shirts and Izod golf skirts that had the cutest little green alligators on it, now known as Lacoste. Who would have known I had already chosen the trendy fashion in golf back then for golf attire. It seemed I was always in fashion due to sports.

I married at the age of 21. In planning my wedding, I found a wonderful bridal shop. The owner Zaida, who was also a seamstress, tailored the perfect white wedding gown for me with a long train with satin buttons up beaded backing. My veil was imported from Spain, trimmed with lace flowing over my dress behind me to the floor, I felt like a fairytale princess. I was happy. My bridesmaids were dressed in chiffon peach southern bell long gowns with hats and white gloves all looking very elegant. What a Fashion Statement!

I was now modeling for a plus size clothing store. I was a size 12 which was considered a plus size. I never imagined I was a model or a large woman. Being an athlete, I seemed to carry a lot of muscle weight. I was able to build up a nice wardrobe.

I then was ready to plan my first baby shower. Wow, she has arrived--- Crystal Summers baby girl fashion. I was now making hand-made satin ribbon lace bows for my daughter and her friends dressing up her catholic plaid uniforms with hair bows. It has a familiarity about it, next generation of fashion. I'm now faced with what you call branding designer labels; keep in mind uniforms up until High School were amazing.

My Crystal ended up at Chapman University for four years. No more uniforms, we are now talking money. Keeping up with the Jones's. Lucky for me I had to work harder for clothing of labels and trends as this generation was all about the Fashion Statement. Each generation changes and somehow repeats itself.

In my work I have many events I personally attend. Some are golf events so for those you will find me in golf attire. I also am an ambassador for the local chamber so depending on the function I dress for that in styles and colors that work for me, I also do and go to many events, so for some of those you will find me in long evening dresses or dressy shorter dresses to fit the occasion. I also have a great selection of casual dresses that I wear during the day when not dressed in my golf attire.

I want to emphasize it's not what you wear, it's how you feel when you step out. Designer labels are amazing if that's how you truly want to represent yourself. You can wear something that makes you feel like a super model and love it!

What's in your heart and deep inside feeling of confidence will always bring you to a higher place as you were made by a higher power and the clothing you wear is your cape of glory and honor.

Be true to yourself. Believe in yourself.

What is your FASHION STATEMENT?

* *

Charmaine Summer is the manager of the Cherry Hills Golf Club in Menifee CA and is a LPGA golf pro, She resides with her husband Freddy and their dog Perris in Menifee, Ca. She lived in Orange County CA for many years and ran the Orange County Gold Academy. Her daughter Crystal and Husband with their children (her grandchildren) live in Pennsylvania.

She is also the director of the Lake Arrowhead Global Society for Female Entrepreneurs Network (GSFE) a 501 c 3 nonprofit, she has won numerous awards over the years including citizen of the month from her city for her work with women and youth. She can be reached at 714-350-3626 text or phone.

Alessandra Thornton

Fashion Is Color And Nature Advocacy

My first fashion influencer was my mother. I remember admiring her dressed in A-line colorful and mod mini dresses paired with colorful bangles, wedges, thick hair bands, and her blonde bob hairstyle.

I wanted to be as beautiful and colorful as she was. My mom always sewed new colorful floral dresses for her five daughters and styled us with that boho hippie chic style of the 70s. Fashion in the 70s was full of color and bold psychedelic patterns. I have grown up with that color explosion that reflects in all the jewelry designs I create.

Let me introduce myself: I am Alessandra Thornton (former name Alessandra Posligua), owner and head designer of Organic Jewelry by Allie. I was born in the tropical city of Guayaquil, Ecuador, a city close to the river, where the young people go out every Friday to the bars to dance under the rhythms of Cumbia, Salsa, and Merengue. We are loud and colorful. We live for today as if there is no tomorrow. The people in the Andes of Ecuador call us "monos" to identify us as noisy, happy, brightly dressed people. We are the version of the Caribbean people.

When I moved to the United States to marry my husband, John Thornton, I never imagined the turn my life was about to take in fashion, and fashion with purpose. I arrived here with 2 bachelor's degrees, one in Journalism, the second in Archeology, and with experience in many magazines, TV channels, and even the Museum of the Central Bank in Ecuador. I thought it would be easy for me to find jobs in my field of expertise right away.

The experience proved me wrong. I ended up volunteering for a while at San Diego Archaeological Center. In Journalism, when the newspapers read my articles, they congratulated my work but asked me: Can you do that work without spelling assistance in English? In those times Grammarly and other AI tools did not exist, so I lost job opportunities.

My first job was in Macy's men's department as a sales-associated clearing the fitting rooms. We were always short-staffed and carrying too many men's suits affected my arm and my shoulder mobility. Eventually it was painful to reach out, lift my arms, and even dress myself. I left work with a disability and dedicated months to rehabilitation therapy.

In the meantime, it was the beginning of eBay, and I heard a lot of people were clearing closets and making money. I taught community adult classes to sell on eBay, imported artisan crafts from Ecuador, and a new income was born in the middle of healing my body. My eBay store is Le Petite Bohemian.

I discovered there was jewelry made of rainforest nuts, made by the company "Bototagua" no longer in business. I fell in love with the eco-friendly idea of organic jewelry and the unique nut prints that make the pieces look like marble.

Fascinated, I decided to discover the town of the artisans who made these kinds of jewels on my next trip;   I found it, which is not even in the signals of the highways in Ecuador, and knocked on the doors of people that were working on the nuts. Can you work on my designs if I bring new fashion ideas for the nuts? Many artisans said yes, which is how my jewelry brand: Organic Jewelry by Allie started.

In Businesses, you cannot be divorced from fairness, community involvement, and giving back.

 On one of those trips, I scheduled a visit to the rainforests where the tagua trees grow. It was one of the worst El Nino seasons. Roads were underwater, crops were lost, and entire towns were isolated from the cities.

While assessing the damage, I discovered only the banana trees and the tagua nut palms were unaffected by the rain. Banana is the first export income in Ecuador.

That was my aha moment, and I decided to dedicate my life to the creation, promotion, and commerce of Tagua nut and rainforest seeds jewelry. Vegan jewelry crafting gives another income to families in rural areas.

 In 2010 I started to show my jewels in every farmer's market around San Diego. Every week, I made five farmers' markets from Chula Vista to Oceanside, besides my online stores on eBay and Etsy. When applying to local art shows, I heard rejections because they wanted jewelry made locally by United States artisans. These rejections gave me more reasons to learn. I traveled back to Ecuador, stayed for one month in an artisan town, and learned to make sustainable jewelry.

Today I release not only naturally sourced but also nature-inspired jewelry. We have many collections: Deep Ocean, Magical Rainforest, Paradise Islands, and Wild&Free, whose wants to create awareness with fashion about rainforest conservation, clean oceans free of plastics for marine life, and the use of nuts as a cruelty-free alternative in tribal jewels, the tagua nut represents the vegan option and can be carved even like the claws or the tusk of an animal, there is not fashion statement in extinction.

We also have two giving back projects, "Operation Girl Empowerment", giving back every year school supplies and pre-owned recycled Barbie dolls to orphan girls in Ecuador, and the "You Rescue Me" collection for pet parents and horse lovers, which gives 30% of the sales in dry food, blankets, and toys to my local animal shelter.

As I said, no business can be divorced from the environment and giving back to the community, and fashion, for me, is creating meaningful, colorful jewels that empower women and preserve rainforest one design at a time, giving the ethnic groups and rural communities, economic reasons to become the first guardians of the rainforests.

You can find many of my designs in many Museum Stores. We are members of the Museum Store Association, at California mission shops and retreat centers all over the USA, and at Faire wholesale; we sell all over the world. But my new creations are posted frequently on my site: Allie Tagua jewelry.

Many Tiki queens are loyal customers; the Tiki world loves the tropical feeling of my jewelry.

We have collaborated with many San Diego and Los Angeles fashion designers who share the vision of creating sustainable, cruelty-free, recycled, and repurposed fashion made in small batches with a minimal carbon footprint. We want to leave our legacy, the message of ethical fashion production for a better world.

Let's start to put Organic Jewelry by Allie in your life and travel to magical paradise places with the true gems of nature: The tagua nuts!

Dr. Joan Wakeland

The Bold, Bling, and Attractive

Fashionista!

It is great to put on nice clothes, but greater than the look is the attitude of the person wrapped in pretty packaging! When you are wearing a nice outfit and your demeanor is great, you feel comfortable, you walk confidently, and doors seem to open quicker. I was a medical sales representative and had to call on doctors, physician assistants, nurses and office staff.

In the early days of my career, I never wore artificial acrylic nails. A Physician Assistant introduced me to the nail shop. My male boss introduced me the salon for makeup lessons. I wore Skirt Suits and nylon hosiery!

I was told that most gatekeepers let you in the door after they judge your appearance. Have you ever felt that you were not allowed to be in a room because of how you were dressed? You were not permitted because someone prejudged you! Snobbery has been in existence since biblical times. The rich man with the gold ring could enter, but the poor vile man was shunned. Check out James 2 verse 1 through 13 if you disagree with me.

This has been my own experience that I am sharing with you. I decided to do my own experiment. I dressed down, I wore no jewelry to enhance my outfit, and I needed to go to the hairdresser the next day, so I wore a hat. The color of my suit was gray, and the blouse was black. That day was a gray day for me. I was denied access to many offices. I thought this was just a coincidence. It's all in my mind, so I did this a few times only to have the same results in different places! I found out that I had a better outcome when I was dressed in colored apparel---something that popped out against my melanin skin. e.g., black with fuchsia, cobalt blue, purple and red!

I also became more aware that when my hair, nails, and makeup were done, that I saw more clients in a day.

While my attire might have helped me get my foot in the door, ultimately my attitude, personality, and knowledge allowed me to be a productive professional representative.

It costs nothing to be kind, and nothing to put a smile on your face. When you have a bad attitude, people don't want to give you the time of day. You may lose out on many opportunities! Unfortunately, you become the wounded victim. So many people do not realize that they are wearing their emotions on their faces. You can see disgust, fear, frown, hate, hostility, and love in the eyes. No wonder the eyes are described as the windows of the soul! Nobody wants or cares to be with someone who wears a mask to cover ugliness! It is therefore important to start your journey with a good attitude! Whatever is the problem, never take it out on others. Learn to not sweat the small stuff; let it go!

My appearance is very important to me. The image that one portrays can say so much about herself. It shows how much you love yourself. It shows how much you care about your appearance. It shows you how much you value yourself! It shows if you are a little bit crazy or not! The day that you felt that you can slip away for a quick visit to the store in your pajamas, house slippers, flip flops, no makeup, and curlers in your hair is the day that you will meet your prospective client, the handsome eligible bachelor that you wanted to date, your best friend who always thought how you looked fabulous or the gossiping Chatty Cathy neighbor! I guarantee it! My mother always said, "Wear good clothes. Look good all the time. Your bedroom clothes will not be the same clothes you wear in the boardroom! You never know who you will meet!"

My clothing is my messenger. I have only time, only one chance for you to make an impression of me! That moment is when we first met! I like to dress up because when I do, I feel good. I do it for myself! I am more concerned with my self-worth and value than what may be perceived of the apparel I choose to wear. My mother always told me to "wear nice clothes and nice underwear". However, she always reminded me of the Golden Rule! "Do unto others, as you would have them do unto you." Simply said, "Treat others like how you want to be treated! Because you are privileged to wear nice clothes, you must not think you are better than others."

What am I going to wear?

That is a daily question. To simplify finding the items, I color coded my closet. It saves me time. I just go to the color section that I want to wear that day. Another tip that I use is to choose what I want to wear the next day before I go to bed. That includes accessories, jewelry, purse, and shoes. In the morning, I just need to concentrate on getting ready to seize the day!

Where am I going?

If I am at the beach, you may find me barefooted in a one-piece blue or black bathing suit enhanced by a thin white lace cover up.

If I am the park, I wear comfortable, colorful tops with black pants or golf shorts!

However, when I am out on business, I like a crisp look. Black and White works best for me.

I wear modest, classic clothing to church. I don't buy too many trendy styles.

When I am out to have fun, I wear Long Skirts, bling tops, dresses with bling, and gowns! I love bling! My accessories are usually ostentatious necklaces and earrings that accentuate my appearance, making me Bold and Attractive!

Dr. Joan E Wakeland, Retired Pharmacist,
Author of "The Run for Freedom "
Amazon #1 Bestseller & International Best Seller
Empowerment Facilitator SWU Workshops
Director, GSFE Riverside Connectors,
Menifee Valley Lions Charter Member
(909) 721-7648
joanewakeland@gmail.com

Dr. Randi D. Ward

Fashion Is Ever Changing; Real Style Is Everlasting

Ever since I was a little girl, fashion has played an important role in my life. I would try on my clothes and pretend I was a fashion designer and mix and match different styles, colors, fabrics, etc. I had no idea if my fashion sense at the age of eight years old was good (or bad), but I always felt beautiful, glamorous, and so grown-up. Often, I would even don a pair of my mother's high heeled shoes and handbags to complete my created outfit, gaze at myself in the mirror, and secretly pretend to be a famous model preparing for the runway.

Being a typical young girl, I loved pink, green, red, purple, yellow, and other bright colors. Wearing them made me feel so alive and energetic. My favorite seasons are spring and summer, so the colors dominate in these seasons bring joy to my heart. Years ago, I took the Color Test so popular at the time to determine my perfect color palette. Yes, you guessed it. I am a "SPRING".

As I became a teenager, I always needed to follow the latest fashion trends. This was a MUST for me. Being shy at this time in my life and lacking self-confidence, I desperately sought acceptance from my peers, so having the most popular designer and latest-stylish fashions made me feel "less "invisible. Being thin with a good figure made it possible for me to wear any popular style. That was a true blessing.

Miniskirts as well as bell bottom jeans and big shirts were the "rage" during my university years. I went from wearing tight skirts so short it was "dangerous" to sit down without being obscene and revealing too much to the world to wearing clothes so baggy none of my body was visible, except my face. I thought I was so COOL. Imaging myself today in a miniskirt makes me "chuckle" out loud though. My legs are not the same as they once were so my miniskirt days are definitely over; comfortable, loose-fitting but still stylish clothes are a major fashion theme in my current daily life when I am home alone.

I also owned and wore a cute collection of Scottish style kilts and Irish cable-knitted sweaters in style during the late 1960s and early 1970s. I loved these because it gave me a small way to proudly "honor" and "display" my Scotch-Irish heritage. Later as an adult, I would travel to Scotland and Ireland and add more adorable sweaters and skirts to my collection. Living in Atlanta, Georgia, for over 33 years, I no longer wear them. Our winters are usually too warm for such heavy wool garments, but I occasionally pull them out of dresser drawers and try them on. Ahhhh! Such happy travel memories!

When I joined the professional world as an educator at the age of 22 years, my fashions changed drastically out of necessity. For the first fifteen years of my career, only suits and dresses were permitted for the classroom. Wearing slacks was a BIG NO NO! I must admit dressing this way since I was not that much older than my high school students during my early teaching years probably created a better classroom environment of respect and credibility for me as their teacher. These clothes did make me feel like a real grown-up lady and no longer that young girl who tried so hard to look grown-up. At this stage in my life, I developed a deep passion/addiction for high heeled shoes, matching handbags, and designer jewelry. Being only 5 ft. 4 in. tall, those 3-to-4-inch-high heels along with my tailored jackets and matching skirts did make me feel powerful and successful. I actually had so many clothes I could wear a different outfit every day of the 180-day school year. Crazy, I know, but it is true. Even my students noticed this. I was known for my "fashions". Female students would ask for my advice when they were picking out Homecoming or Prom dresses. I felt honored to advise them on what I thought would be stunning on them.

I also started my collection of fine jewelry in Sterling Silver; 14k, 18k, and 24k gold in various colors; and platinum. I own diamonds in almost every color and almost every gemstone known to mankind. I also have a huge loose gemstone collection. Since June is my birth month, pearls and lots of them are a must. No outfit would be complete without the perfect jewelry accessories: necklace(s), bracelet(s), rings, earrings, and watch. As a lady who considers herself a fashionista, I have jewelry for every outfit and for every occasion. My jewelry depicts who I am loudly and clearly---a lady who loves the finer things in life and loves to sparkle wearing my "bling". My jewelry makes me feel glamorous and beautiful. Over many decades, I saved my money and bought my unique and special pieces of jewelry on sale or at wholesale prices when possible. I could now literally open my own jewelry boutique and fill it completely with just my jewelry alone. Wearing a Size 5 or 6 ring, and a Size 7 to 7 ¼ inch bracelet would be helpful for my customers though.

As I grew older and my body was not as thin as it once was, lots of black color was added to my wardrobe. Whether it is actually true or not, I always feel thinner when I wear a black dress, pants, top, or jacket. Of course, a touch of color with a floral scarf or pearls or colored gemstones brightens up my ensemble for a more polished and sophisticated look. Being a blonde with fair skin, I always feel I need some color.

I retired from all classroom teaching after completing a three-month ESOL Contract in Cairo, Egypt, in 2011-12. The "professional" clothes no longer needed were neatly (and sadly) stored away in closets and drawers and over the past 10+ years have been gradually donated to charities. I transitioned to jeans, leggings, casual slacks, tunic tops, light-weight sweaters---a much more casual lifestyle. I am now a professional writer and master editor, so my work is done at my home in my office on my laptop for many hours a day, so "comfort" is essential even though my outfits must be cute and inspire me to do my best work. However, now I only dress up in my highest fashion style for those special events: Award Galas, Fancy Parties, Lunch and Dinner Dates with friends, and Theater Events.

Looking back at the last 74 years of my life, I marvel at how much my fashion has changed and evolved. I still love clothes. I still want to wear some of the new trends when they are appropriate for my body and my age. However, I still hold onto many of the classical styles that never really go out of style. Knowing what my personality is and who I am and recognizing what is now flattering on my mature body now dictate the fashion I happily wear.

By the way, I bought two of Dr. Chebra's gorgeous dresses from photos only. They fit perfectly and are definitely my style. I love them. Dr. Chebra highly recommended them to me. She is a "Genius Designer" and cares so much about her clients. I hope one day to visit her California Boutique.

Dr. Randi D. Ward is an Educator, Book Coach/Master Editor, Co-Owner of RM Infinite, Chancellor of World University of Leadership and Management, Former Owner of 2 Egyptian Language Centers, Best-Selling Author, World Traveler, IAOTP's Female Visionary/Educator of the Decade with 2 Honorary Doctorates (Humanitarianism), USA Presidential

Volunteer Service Lifetime Achievement Award, 100 Successful Women Award and a proud Advisory Board Member, Woman of the Year---Writing/ Language Arts (Top 100 Registry), Nelson Mandela Humanitarian Award, She Inspires Me Award and its Special Love Award, Super Hero Award, Egypt's World Peace Forest (Africa) Honorary President, Kenya's Africa Nomads Conservation USA Director, IIU World Record---Inspirational Woman, 2023 IAOTP Top Global Impact Influencer, and many other awards/honors.

randiteach@yahoo.com
rminfinite1@gmail.com
www.randidward.com
1 678 634 0069

mplete!
GSFE
Global Society for Female Entrepreneurs
CONNECT
COMMUNITY
GSFE
GSFE
Global Society for
Female Entrepreneurs
WELLNESS
INSPIRE
GSFE
Global Society for
Female Entrepreneurs
EMPOW
GSFE
INSPIRE
GSFE
Global Society for
Female Entrepreneurs
GSFE
Global Society for
Female Entrepreneurs

Dr. Violet Williams

A Fashionable Style

What am I wearing a Spiritual side of Fashion.

When I think of this statement, I must go back to my childhood where I believe it all began.

As I reminisce about my childhood, one particular aspect stands out vividly in my memories: my profound love for clothes. It was a fascination that seemed to sprout from the very core of my being, intertwining itself with my identity and shaping the person I would become. Reflecting on those years, I realize that my affinity Love for fashion may have stemmed from a unique combination of circumstances that were directly tied to my physical appearance and creative upbringing. I was extremely thin and so many names were given to me such as toothpick, skinny mini, and spaghetti. That being said, it was so hard to find clothes that fit me; however, I was blessed with a mother who was an amazing seamstress. She could sew without a pattern and would make the most unique elegant dresses and outfits for me.

At the time I was in a dance group called the Kool Kats. There were four of us girls; I was the youngest. My mother took on the role of our costume designer; she created all our outfits for our performance. We performed at the White House, Carnegie Hall, festivals, and dance competitions within New York. Our costumes were so flashy and matched each of our personalities. So not only did we look amazing, but our dance routines were dynamic. Being the youngest, I always stood out. I would hear the crowd say look at that little girl go. I felt the most free and beautiful when I performed.

My fashion sense followed me all through school. In middle school. I was a runner up for best-dressed; however, in high school, I nailed it. I was voted most likely to design her own clothes and best- dressed. I designed all my senior outfits for each event. The showstopper was my prom dress design. I had a professional seamstress bring it to life. It was a showstopper. The colors were pink, lavender, and purple. I felt so beautiful in it; even more, the fact that I created the design made me glow from within.

My love for fashion led me to modeling school. I modeled for several years, and then you guessed it, went to Fashion design school in Los Angeles. I worked at the California Mart in downtown Los Angeles to be surrounded by what I love most---clothes, fabrics, fashion, and the latest design for the season.

Then the infamous day came when I went to look for the ultimate dress---my wedding dress. I searched high and low to find the perfect dress that would exude elegance, beauty virtue, and class and connect to my soul. Expressions of love. I found it. I wanted my bridesmaid to look just as beautiful and elegant to complement me. The designer at this address was Jessica McClintock. Which brings me to the picture of me in this book. I am wearing a Jessica McClintock dress. You may think it's just another beautiful dress. When I first saw the dress, I knew I had to have it. I did not know that designer. The dress was the exact color and style I had imagined and a perfect fit.

I decided to wear it for a GSFE event. I was asked to be one of the entertainers as a singer. When the CEO of GSFE Dr. Robbie Motter asked me to sing, my heart dropped. She had no idea that singing was a deep desire of mine, I sang in the choir, and in a gospel group, but never as a solo singer. I wanted to say yes, but out of fear I tried to decline by explaining to her I am a dancer---not a solo singer. However, I believe that there is no other excitement than fulfilling another one of my dreams. The dress that my bridesmaid wore on my wedding day and the dress that I wore singing solo for the first time at the event have all to do of God's way to spiritually guide me to make the connection that His love for me along with my mother's love was present to reveal to me. But what I wore connected me to my desires, my dreams. I felt empowered, confident, and beautiful. I belted out the most amazing song by Jill Scott, living my life like it's golden and looking amazing while doing so.

Fashion is often seen as a mere expression of personal style, a way to showcase our individuality and creativity. However, there is a deeper, spiritual aspect to fashion that goes beyond superficial trends and appearances. For me, fashion is a sacred journey of self-expression and creativity, a means to connect with my inner being and a way to radiate positive energy and gratitude to the world around me from my best spirit.

Dorothy Wolous

Fashion Sensation

In a world where fast fashion dominates, it's refreshing to see individuals take a sustainable approach to fashion by shopping at thrift stores. Meet Dorothy, a fashion sensation who has made a name for herself by shopping at thrift stores. Dorothy has worked in the business environment all her life, but her passion for fashion is evident in the way she dresses. Her wardrobe is a collection of unique pieces that she has curated from thrift stores.

Dorothy's journey into thrift shopping started when she was broke, had 3 kids to dress, and changed careers. She needed to look presentable for job interviews but had a limited budget. So, she turned to thrift stores, and she was amazed at the selection of high-quality clothing at affordable prices. She found designer pieces that were a fraction of the cost of buying them new. She was hooked. The thrill of finding these hidden gems kept her coming back for more.

As Dorothy started her new career, she continued to shop at thrift stores. She found that the pieces she bought were not only affordable but also unique. She could create her own style by mixing and matching pieces from different eras and styles. She learned that fashion is not about following trends but about expressing yourself and feeling confident in your own skin.

Dorothy's love for thrift shopping has added to her ability to go places she never thought possible. She has attended the Hollywood Emmy's, Oscars, and numerous award shows, all in gowns bought at thrift stores. Her confidence in her personal style has made her thrive to always look fabulous. And believe it or not people are always eager to see what she wears next. She is never ashamed to say where she bought her outfit.

Dorothy's success has inspired others to take a sustainable approach to fashion. Thrift stores have become more popular as people realize the impact of fast fashion on the environment. Dorothy has shown that you don't need to break the bank to look stylish. By shopping at thrift stores, you can save money and still look great.

Dorothy's story is a testament to the power of confidence and individual style. She has shown that you can become a fashion sensation by shopping at thrift stores. Thrift shopping is not only affordable but also a sustainable approach to fashion. It allows you to express yourself and create a unique style that is true to who you are. Dorothy's journey is a reminder that fashion is not about following trends but about being yourself and feeling confident in your own skin.

I know because I am Dorothy. Let me also share that it is relaxing to browse for my next new "find" to rock. The thrill of the hunt brings me such joy; seriously, as funny as it sounds, shopping at a thrift store is so much fun! We now know it's affordable and fun, but on certain days they even give more discounts. Different stores have different discounts, such as Senior day 30% off your entire purchase. Some have $1.00 days; discount on certain color tags will be 50% off; the discounts can be endless. When I take advantage of the discounts, one of my favorite lines when I find a dress or article is" How can I not? It's almost FREE! I must buy it."

I love thrift stores. You, too, could become your own fashion sensation. Rock it!

MOM, Grandma
New Hub Auto Service
Advanced Emission Specialist
Rippin Disc Golf
GSFE-Globalsocietyforfemaleentrepreneurs.com
Fabulous DIVA
International Best-Selling Author
Minister

Cell: (951) 240-0219 | Dorothy.Wolons@yahoo.com

Queen Corazon Ugalde Yellen

From a Beauty Queen and Model's Perspective

I have been a model since I was 13 years old, so fashion is my lifetime passion! It has always been my unique self-expression. I remember as a little girl I would go with my grandma Brigida shopping for my clothes for school or special occasions like birthday parties. We would go to a local shopping center or shopping mall, and I knew what I wanted. I would pick dresses with printed flowers or ribbons with matching bag and shoes. Pink or pastel colors are my favorites. I always love feminine, sweet looks.

I was born and raised in Metro Manila, Philippines. My father, Aurelio Sipin Ugalde was a Brigadier General of the Philippine Air Force and Vice President of Feati University. My mother was a loving housewife and mother of six children. I have 3 sisters and two brothers. I was the youngest girl, second to the youngest. Among 28 grandchildren, on my mother's side, I was the favorite grandchild of my grandma Brigida Lucero. So, you can imagine, I love to go shopping for clothes and toys with my sweetest grandma in the world!

When I was 10 years old, my oldest sister Cynthia won the Miss Philippines beauty pageant and also became a model and actress. Growing up, she was one of my inspirations when it comes to beauty and fashion. Both my grandma and my mom were fashionistas, too. At 13 years old, I was chosen to do a print ad and TV Commercials for Pepsi Cola! I was thrilled! I wore the most fashionable, cool outfit that a teenager would die for! Walking the runway, doing the catwalk, modeling for two well-known Fashion Designers Goulee Gorozpe and Emil Valdez at The Hyatt Hotel when I was 14 years old was a dream come true! I loved the way Haute Couture High Fashion gowns LOOK on me! It made me feel so special. I felt like a Real Princess!

In those days, I was rebellious, so I eloped and married my boyfriend when I was only 18 years old. I have been married 4 times. From Manila, Philippines, I moved to Oslo, Norway, New York City, and Los Angeles, California, where I reside now with my significant other Frank. My daughter Bridgette Yellen Rosenberg, who is also a model and a fashionista, and son Sean Yellen, along with my 3-year-old granddaughter Sophie and 7-year-old grandson Charles Yellen, all live in Los Angeles. My family is my greatest achievement in Life and the Love of my Life!

Through the years, I had many careers. I am a real estate agent, fashion and commercial model, actress, author and multi titled beauty queen. When I won several beauty queen titles, I wore exquisite, beautiful gowns by well-known Fashion Designers; among them is Celebrity Fashion Designer Chebra Dorsey of Ochea Fashion. I walked the runway for her, and I wore Ochea Fashion on several of my International Magazine Covers as the Cover Girl. I love Ochea Fashion because it looks fabulous on me! Her fashion makes me feel a complete woman. It is unique, avant garde and exquisite! I love dresses that make me feel the very best I can be, both physically and spiritually. To be an inspiration to the younger generation. I attend several Red-Carpet events and Charity affairs, and I make sure I wear my beautiful crown and sash, favorite gown, accessories like sparkly diamonds and fabulous shoes! I am currently the Ms Asia France International 2023, World Class Beauty Queen USA Ambassador, World Class Woman of the Year, World Class Legend, Ms Amerasia International, Ms Global America World, Noble Queen of the Universe Classic, Ms Asia Glamour, Mrs Asia USA California, Ms Travel of the World, Ms Paris International Universe, Mrs Philippines, Mrs Cultural World Philippines, Ms Intercontinental Universe, Ms Gandang Pilipina USA, Ms All Women Rock Global Elite, Ms Love of Country Travel and Trade Ambassador, Ms Fashion Queen, Ms Noble Global Model, Princess of the Universe Ambassador, Queen of Queens, and Ms Icon Queen of the Decade among others.

It was thrilling to model for a major mannequin manufacturer Greneker Company in Los Angeles, California. They took a face mold of my face in 2 versions, one slightly smiling, and the other with a big happy smile. For another version, I sat for an artist to sculpt my face on clay with no smile. All three versions become mannequins to be sold in Department Stores and Boutiques in the USA, Asia, and Europe. It was a wonderful experience and so awesome to see my" Corazon model mannequin" in Department stores like Macy's – immortalized as an Asian Mannequin worldwide, wearing the latest coolest fashion! The sample mannequin they gave me is now standing in my doll collection room. I dress my mannequin in different wonderful fashions. I love creating incredible looks for my own mannequin at home.

One of my hobbies is collecting all kinds of dolls. Some of my favorites are Barbie dolls! Barbie is the Queen of Fashion! I admire all her fashions through the years! I was the Founder and President of The Beverly Hills Barbie Doll Club, and I had Barbie collector members all over the world! We had regular meetings about our common interests as Barbie collectors. I organized a Barbie Fashion Show, and it was held at the famed Queen Mary Ballroom in Long Beach, California. We donated proceeds from the Mini Convention and Fashion Show to different Charity groups. For many years, I walked the runway, doing the catwalk, modeling Life Sized Barbie Fashionable outfits for several Barbie Conventions in the USA and Germany. I was named "The Living Doll" and have been featured in several publications all over the world, wearing a life-sized Barbie Fashion! I was a guest of the Phil Donahue Show, The Mo Gaffney Talk Show and The Roseanne Barr TV Show. I was interviewed by the late legendary Dick Clark during his TV game show-

It takes Two. It was an amazing experience! I felt like a Barbie Doll with fabulous fashions on her fingertips!

As an actress, I had many interesting roles in stage plays, musical plays, television TV series, TV movies. and films! Wearing the right wardrobe and fashion puts me on point with my character. I had glamorous, dramatic and comedic roles. For my lead role as Queen Puso in the musical play, The Legend of Queen Puso, I had two different roles. I wore 16th Century costumes as an Asian Queen. My costumes were beautiful golden rich brocades with exquisite jewelry and crown. I was reincarnated as a modern woman in the 20th century with modern wardrobe and fashionable attires. I won Best Actress as a poor, rebellious prostitute during civil war in the dramatic Stage play "There was a Soldier". It was my recollection of my encounter with this particular soldier in the midst of the war. My wardrobe was a simple, sexy lingerie with a robe and this wardrobe brought out the bitterness, love, and anger of this young woman.

I have travelled to 100 countries in the world, the seven continents, and the seven wonders of the World! Whenever I travel, I change my fashion everyday according to the mood and beauty of the magical place. When I walked the Great Walls of China, I felt the beauty and the grandeur of this amazing place. I wore a fashionable yellow gold dress, that emoted opulence and wonder! Another wonder of the world is The Treasury in Petra, Jordan. The hand-carved sandstone Treasury building is one of the most famous archaeological sites, so I wore a hand beaded top with an exotic head piece. This place was magical and one of my favorite places on earth! Wearing an exotic fashion made me feel I belonged there! I felt the spirituality of this truly magical place!

So, for me, Fashion is my lifestyle. I am a Fashionista forever! By Queen Corazon Ugalde Yellen

Queen Corazon Ugalde Yellen

Follow Instagram - @BeautyQueenCorazonYellen

Facebook – Queen Corazon Ugalde Yellen

TikTok - @QueenCorazon22

YouTube Channel – Beauty Queen Corazon Ugalde Yellen Armenta

Email -

corayellen@aol.com

Hair
make-up
O'CHEA
FASHION BOUTIQUE
FASHION
MORE IS
MORE
SEASON
A Dress
for every
Occasion
Beauty - Fashion

DESIGN BY O'CHEA

MRS ASIA GLAM

ESIGN BY O'CHEA

9 798989 191857